Donna Parker

A SPRING TO REMEMBER

By
MARCIA MARTIN

Illustrated by
SARI

WHITMAN PUBLISHING COMPANY
RACINE, WISCONSIN

Donna Parker's head started to throb, and the telephone shook in her hand. The news she had just received would change the course of her friend Ricky West's life— and her own as well.

It was only the first of the trying situations which she was to face during that eventful spring. Ahead loomed graduation, and the unexpected competition for the Outstanding Girl Award. There was the question of a summer vacation in California—could that dream possibly come true? And then there was her part in Bunny's wedding— an experience that would haunt Donna as long as she lived.

Somewhere within herself Donna had to find real wisdom to meet the problems of growing up. She had to find the loyalty to stand by Ricky when bitter resentment threatened to end their friendship forever, and understanding to help handsome, blond Paul when he turned to her in desperation. Each new day brought its challenge, exciting and disturbing, until Donna was certain that above all others this had become *A Spring to Remember*.

CONTENTS

CHAPTER 1

A Telephone Call

"Don't touch a single thing until I get back," called dark-haired Donna Parker over her shoulder, as she ran down the stairs to answer the telephone. "I'll only be a minute, and I don't want to miss anything."

"Aw, gee!" She could hear her little brother's wail. "Do we have to wait for her, Mom? Do we, Dad?"

She hoped it wasn't Ricky West on the phone. Even though Ricky was Donna's best friend, this was no time for one of their long conversations—not when Mr. and Mrs. Parker had just this morning returned from a fabulous month-long trip to India, and she had hardly had a chance to hear about it. Probably Ricky wanted to discuss plans for the spring vacation which had just begun. Well, she would simply tell Ricky to call back later!

"Hello?" she said, still listening to make sure nothing

11

was happening upstairs. But her attention was centered completely on the telephone when an unfamiliar masculine voice at the other end said, "Grace?"

"No," replied Donna demurely. "This is not Mrs. Parker. It is her daughter, Donna." Who would know that her mother had just gotten into the house?

There was a deep chuckle. "My, my, you're so formal, Donna! Don't you recognize your uncle's voice?"

Donna gasped. "Why—why, it's Uncle Roger! Where are you? Are you calling from California? Are you here in Summerfield? How did you know that Mommy's home?"

"Not so fast, young lady. No, I'm not in California, and I'm not in Summerfield, either. I'm in New York on business, and I missed meeting your mother and father at the boat by just a few minutes. An important call detained me—"

"Oh, Uncle Roger," Donna interrupted. "We were there, and we'd have loved to see you. Oh, I know Mommy and Daddy will be so disappointed. Wait, I'll call them to the phone."

"Now hold on, young lady," Roger Norcross laughed. "Maybe you can give your mother a message instead. If you'll all be home this afternoon, I might be able to take the train out, and spend a little while with you before I catch my midnight plane back to the coast. And I have something special to discuss with you too."

"Would you? Could you? Ooh, that would be wonderful. I'll tell Mommy right away. 'By!"

Donna raced up the steps to her parents' bedroom. Sure enough, everything was just as she had left it.

"Gee, it looks almost like Christmas morning," she thought happily. Half to herself she asked, "Now where did I put the presents you brought me?"

"Right here where you were sitting, dear," Mrs. Parker said, pointing to a pile of silk scarves, ivory fans, sandalwood figurines, and Indian dolls. "And be awfully careful of that French perfume, Cooky. It's almost as expensive in Paris as it is here."

"Now, where were we?" Donna asked, putting all her souvenirs in her lap, and thinking of the expressions on the faces of her friends when they saw all these gorgeous, glamorous things.

"Well," said Mr. Parker, "first I'd like to know who was on the telephone."

Donna bit her lip. "Goodness," she sighed. "The minute a new thought pops into my head, the last one pops right out. I came up here to tell you about the phone call, and then . . . " she shook her head sadly.

"Old age, that's all," offered her eight-year-old brother Jimmy. "That's what happens when you get to be fourteen. She's wearin' out fast, I can tell you. You should have seen her when you was away, Mom—"

"*Were* away, smartie," mumbled Donna.

Mrs. Parker laughed, "Now I really feel I'm back. When you two start badgering each other, it seems that I've never left home. But what about the phone call, Donna?"

"It was Uncle Roger, Mommy." She stopped in order to watch her mother's face.

"My brother? He called from California? Donna, do you mean he's been waiting on the phone all this time? Oh, how could you?" Mrs. Parker started quickly out of the room.

"Come back, Mommy," Donna called after her. "He's not on the phone now. And he wasn't calling from California. He was calling from New York. And he hung up."

"Oh, Donna, how could you?" Mrs. Parker repeated. "Why didn't you let me talk to him?"

"Because he's coming here this afternoon," Donna answered. She delivered his message. Then she recalled his last words. Something special to be discussed with her? She could almost feel her heart turn over. When Uncle Roger was around, exciting things always happened. What could he have meant?

Mrs. Parker was bustling about the bedroom. "I'll be so glad to see Roger. Come on, Donna, let's get this mess straightened up."

Donna nodded. "I'll take my things into my room. And, Jimmy, you get the big wastebasket and put all these papers in it."

Jimmy turned to his mother. "See? See what I mean, Mom? There she goes givin' orders again. You tell her to clean up, and right away she's tellin' *me* to get the wastebasket."

"Jimmy!" Mr. Parker said sharply. Then his tone softened. "Please, not on our very first day back. All the time we were away we kept thinking of what wonderful children we had, and how proud we were of you, and kept showing your pictures to everyone."

"You did?" Jimmy asked in a tone of unbelief. He sauntered out into the hall. "I'll be back in a minute, Dad— I think the wastebasket's in my room."

"I suppose Roger will stay to dinner," Mrs. Parker said

to her husband. "He's traveled so much himself, I know he'll want to hear all about the trip." Then she turned to her daughter. "I certainly am glad this is the beginning of Easter vacation, Donna, and you'll be home from school for a while. It's been so long since I've done any cooking, I'm not sure I know how to get a meal together. You'll have to help me."

"Oh, of course, Mommy. Let's make it a real company dinner!" After all, Uncle Roger was a very special guest. "I'll be downstairs in just a minute."

Donna carried her souvenirs into her room. Then she leaned both elbows on the top of her chest of drawers, looking dreamily at her image in the mirror. To think that only a few months ago she had met her mother's youngest brother for the first time. He lived so far away, and had had so little to do with the family for such a long time.

Of course, he hadn't been married then. It had been sheer luck that he had happened to visit the Parkers when Donna's teacher, Miss Fischer, came to dinner. And Donna, with all her romantic ideas, had never even realized that they had fallen in love until they told her that they were getting married!

It had been so wonderful when Uncle Roger and her new

aunt, as they left Summerfield, had invited her out to California. There had been nothing definite, of course. But they had said that as soon as they were settled, she would be one of their first guests.

"Donna!" Mrs. Parker called. "I thought you were going to help me with the dinner."

"In one minute, Mommy." The dark-haired girl stared at her reflection in the mirror.

Uncle Roger had said that he had something to discuss with her, hadn't he? And he had also said that he was taking a midnight flight back to the Coast tonight, hadn't he? Suppose, just suppose, that the real reason why he was making the trip to Summerfield, aside from seeing her parents, of course, was to get their permission to let her go to California this very night! She could spend the entire Easter vacation there, and come back when school reopened.

Suppose this very night her fairy godfather (Uncle Roger) whisked her off in a magic coach (one of those huge, super de luxe airliners), and she went flying through the clouds to an enchanted land (California), perhaps to meet her royal prince. Midnight! Just like Cinderella, only the spell would begin when the clocks chimed twelve, instead of ending then.

And how could her parents refuse, when they had just returned from such an exciting trip themselves? They would have to say Yes! Certainly her mother could do the cooking by herself if she wanted to—she had only been teasing. Imagine, the whole vacation in California—seeing movie stars, swimming in the Pacific Ocean, visiting a part of the country she had heard so much about!

"Please, Mommy," Donna called, running out of her room and into the front bedroom. "Please, please say Yes."

CHAPTER 2   *Uncle Roger's Promise*

"Whatever are you talking about, Donna?" asked Mrs. Parker, who was busily transferring dresses from suitcase to closet. "Say Yes to what?"

Donna stopped short at the doorway to her parents' bedroom. Say Yes to what? To a trip that she had not yet been asked to take, to a trip that (she sighed) she might *never* be asked to take? Goodness, she was always accusing Ricky West of going off on flights of fancy, of letting her imagination run wild and dreaming all sorts of impossible things. Now she was doing the same thing, and almost believing her dreams were real.

"Oh, nothing, Mommy. I was just thinking that Uncle Roger . . ." her voice trailed off.

Mrs. Parker looked up from her unpacking, her arms filled with clothes. Then she sank down on the nearest chair and looked at Donna's face carefully.

"You're still thinking of the trip to California that Uncle Roger mentioned, aren't you, Cooky?"

Donna nodded.

"I know how much you want to go, dear. And Daddy and I would love to have you go, especially since we enjoyed our own trip so much." Mrs. Parker hesitated, as though trying to find the right words. "But you know that Uncle Roger is a very busy man. He may have forgotten that he ever said anything about a trip to California, even though you took the remark so seriously."

"But—but—" Donna began. Then she blurted out, "But, Mommy, suppose he has remembered? Suppose he does ask me? May I say Yes?" The words came out in a rush. "It wouldn't take me any time at all to pack."

Mrs. Parker looked at Donna, then startled her daughter by laughing. "Honey, now really! You couldn't possibly mean that you expect to go tonight!"

"Why not?" Donna insisted.

"It's completely out of the question," Mrs. Parker stated firmly. "A long trip like that—and you'd have to be back in a week or so, when school begins. Doesn't it sound a little ridiculous, even to you?"

Donna turned around, her head drooping. It had seemed too good to be true.

"While we're on the subject, Donna, I'd like to say something more."

Now what? the girl thought.

"It's just possible that Uncle Roger might invite you to come to California this summer, when school has ended."

Of course, Donna thought. Most likely that was what he would do. And she wouldn't mind waiting until then, though leaving tonight would have been more exciting.

"You know, dear," Mrs. Parker was saying, "that Daddy and I would love never to refuse you anything. But as you can well imagine, our trip was quite expensive, and we spent far more for gifts to bring home than we planned."

"You—you mean that even if Uncle Roger asked me, I couldn't go? Even if it didn't cost anything while I'm out there? Just the airline ticket, and you say *that* would be too much money? Is that what you mean, Mommy?"

Mrs. Parker tried to be consoling. "The ticket alone would be several hundred dollars, dear. I'm sure you understand that." Then her voice changed. "But there doesn't seem to be any sense in discussing tickets at this point. Uncle Roger hasn't even mentioned the subject."

She looked at her watch. "Gracious, I'd better hurry. At the rate I'm going, Uncle Roger will be here and I won't be nearly ready."

Donna walked slowly back to her room. She wasn't going to argue with her mother on her first day back. But that couldn't stop her from thinking things, could it? All that money for some stupid presents which had been sent by ship, and wouldn't get here for three or four months, and which she probably wouldn't want anyhow. And those stupid things they had brought home—silly carved figures, and that dopey wooden boat for Jimmy, and all that other junk. Why had she ever thought the gifts were gorgeous and glamorous? And now there wasn't enough money for one little ticket to California!

She sat up and picked at some loose threads on the bed-spread. Well, maybe she was being just a teeny-weeny bit mean. After all, her parents wouldn't have many more chances to travel. Goodness, they were practically forty years old—the best part of their lives behind them—so she couldn't really begrudge them their one trip.

But she wasn't getting any younger either, and she wanted to live a little too. She sighed. She did want to go to California so badly. Maybe something would happen to make it possible. Maybe she would win a contest, or hold the lucky number in a raffle, or have someone she never heard of leave her money so that she could buy the ticket herself. She went down the stairs slowly, lost in thought.

"What are you mooning about now?" Mrs. Parker asked, as Donna gave her a box of bread crumbs instead of salt.

"I'm sorry, Mommy," Donna apologized. Goodness, she had better stop dreaming. After all, she did want Uncle Roger to enjoy his meal.

The dinner preparations had just been concluded when there was a heavy tread on the front porch, and the doorbell rang.

"Uncle Roger!" Donna breathed. "Wasn't that perfect timing?" She whipped off her apron and ran to the door.

But Jimmy had gotten there before her, and a tall, well-dressed man, with dark hair and dark eyes like her own, was standing in the front hall.

Suddenly shyness overtook Donna. Quite unexpectedly she realized that, after all, she didn't know her mother's youngest brother very well.

Roger Norcross, however, seemed very much at ease.

"Donna!" he cried, holding her off at arm's length so that he could take a good look at her. "You haven't changed

at all—just as pretty as you used to be."

Donna blushed. "How's—" What should she call her new aunt? "How's your wife?" she finally asked.

"Adele sends her love to all of you," Mr. Norcross said. "And, Donna, did you know that she insisted on going back to teaching? She says that it's because housekeeping takes up so little of her time. But I think it's because she misses you and all your young friends. She can't wait until you can come out to visit us this summer."

Donna drew in her breath. So they hadn't forgotten the invitation! She caught her mother's eye and looked at her pleadingly. But Mrs. Parker shook her head.

Mr. Norcross turned to his sister. "Grace, you've hardly said a word. Tell me all about your trip—the Orient is one part of the world I've always wanted to see. Sam, you must have brought back some snapshots." He clapped his brother-in-law on the shoulder. "Hand them over."

Mr. Parker chuckled. "Now that's a request I won't hear very often. I'm sure most people, when they see me coming, will say, 'Here comes that bore with his pictures again. Let's get out of his way fast.' But since you insist . . . ."

Mr. Parker dug into his jacket pocket and brought out a small folder which he handed to Mr. Norcross.

"Let me see too," cried Jimmy, trying to elbow his way in front of his sister. "I want to see the pitchers."

"Pic-tures!" hissed Donna. "If you can't say it right, you won't see them at all."

She realized that she was taking out her disappointment on Jimmy. But she had to scold someone. How dreadful to be offered such a lovely vacation and have to refuse it!

She knew that look of her mother's, though. The matter was ended.

Ended, that is, until Uncle Roger said good-by.

"Remember, Donna," he said as he squeezed her hand, "we're expecting to see you as soon as school is over. You're finishing ninth grade now, if I recall correctly."

Donna started to offer some sort of excuse. But her uncle raised his hand to stop her.

"Now, not another word," he said. "You're to come right after your junior high commencement and stay as long as you like. Your ticket will be our graduation present."

Donna's mouth opened. She blinked her eyes to keep away the tears that were forming, but she was too stunned to speak. Was she going to get her ticket, after all?

"Roger!" gasped Mrs. Parker. "How very sweet of you. If you only knew how much this means to Donna! Aren't you happy, dear? Say something."

"I—I can't talk."

Mr. Parker strode into the hall. "Car's ready, Roger. Come on, don't want to miss your train." Then he looked at the little group. "Good heavens, what's happened now?"

Mrs. Parker explained, and Mr. Parker laughed. "Donna looks as though a thunderbolt had struck her. Come on, girl." He snapped his fingers. "Wake up, wake up."

Then he turned to Mr. Norcross and shook his finger, smiling. "See what you've done now, Rog, old boy? Put my daughter in a complete trance. Six more weeks till she graduates, and do you think she'll get one minute's worth of studying done? Nope, either she'll be mooning over what clothes to take, or dreaming about movie stars."

"What have I done now?" Mr. Norcross said, taking his brother-in-law quite seriously. "You mean if she does poorly at school it'll be my fault?" He shook his head.

Then he turned to his niece. "Donna, you can't put me in a position like this. I'd never forgive myself. Tell you what—I'll make a bargain with you. We'll show your father that he's all wrong about your studying. I'll bet that you get the best report you've ever had. In fact, I'll bet your ticket to California that you get all *A*'s." He pointed a finger at her. "Hear? The minute I get a letter saying that you've received all *A*'s, I'll send out your round-trip ticket immediately." He took her hand. "You can do it, Donna. I'm sure you can." Then he winked. "That'll show your father that old Uncle Roger is a good influence."

Donna nodded silently. On her last report she had gotten *A*'s in everything but algebra, and if she worked a little harder, certainly she could pull up that one mark. She took a deep breath, then smiled and nodded again.

"I'm sure I can too, Uncle Roger." She would simply have to get all *A*'s! And with a trip to California to work for, nothing would stop her. She wouldn't *let* anything stop her!

Ricky! She must call Ricky and tell her immediately. They hadn't spoken to each other all day, and now she had this wonderful, marvelous news to tell her.

Come to think of it, why hadn't Ricky called? It was strange—usually they talked several times a day.

"Hello, Ricky?" She could hardly contain her excitement. "You'll never guess what!"

"Oh, Donna, I'm so glad you called," Ricky said, in a voice so low that Donna could hardly hear her. "Something awful has happened. Oh, Donna, I'm so scared!"

CHAPTER 3   *Richard and Ricky*

"But—but listen!" Donna said, her voice dropping almost as low as Ricky's. She simply had to tell Ricky about California.

Then she stopped. Ricky really had sounded scared; this was not one of her play-acting scenes.

"Whatever has happened?" Donna whispered, not knowing why. "Can you talk?"

Was that a sniffle she heard? "Just for a minute, Don. You see, my mother hasn't been feeling well, and today the doctor came and said she had to stay in bed, and not even get out for meals, and my father won't be home until later tonight."

"Is she really very sick, Ricky? Do you want me to come and stay with you until your father comes home?"

This time the sniffle was more pronounced. "That's—

that's just the trouble, Don. I don't mind taking care of Mother. I gave her juices all day, and some soup, and the medicines that the doctor left. It's not my mother that's bothering me so much. It's my father."

"Your father?" Donna repeated, mystified. "Is he sick too?"

Somehow this remark seemed to cheer Ricky. "No, silly," she answered. "He's perfectly well—physically, I mean."

"Ricky!" Donna was shocked. "Are you telling me that there's something else wrong with your father?"

This time Ricky actually giggled. "Of course not." Then her tone became somber again. "But he's so *difficult*. He's not like your father at all," she said wistfully.

What could she say? Donna wondered. She knew just what Ricky meant. Mr. West was so pompous, so solemn and formal, that everyone found it difficult to say anything in his presence. He never joked with Ricky, the way her father did, or came over and gave her a bear hug, or even called her *honey* or *sweetie*.

"But he's nobody to be scared of," Donna protested. "After all, he is your father."

"Know something?" Ricky replied. "I can't even carry on a conversation with him. In fact, I won't even let him drive me to school when he offers, because I'm so miserable for the whole ride thinking of something to say."

"Oh, Ricky!" Imagine having a father you couldn't talk to, or kid with. "Well, maybe this will be the best way to make friends. While your mother is in bed, you and your father will have to have your meals together, and maybe you'll become better friends."

"That's another thing," Ricky whispered. "Father is so particular about his food. And I don't know anything at all about cooking. Could—could you help me a little tomorrow, Donna?"

"Sure thing. The minute I finish with my work here, I'll be right over. Don't worry, Ricky. Everything will be all right," she consoled her friend.

"I think Mother's calling. I'd better run." Ricky hung up suddenly, and Donna remained standing by the phone. Poor Ricky! She hoped Mrs. West would get better very quickly.

Donna jumped as the telephone rang. It must be Ricky calling back, she thought.

But a faintly familiar boy's voice said, "Hello, Donna?"

"Who is it?" she asked, trying to recall where she had heard the voice before.

"It's Richard White. Do you remember me?"

Of all people! She had never really expected him to call.

"Certainly," she said. "Your orchestra played for our ninth grade Spring Dance just before vacation began. And for tenth grade boys, they're really very good, Richard."

"Well, I'm glad you think so, Donna—not everyone agrees about that. But at least it's a way to earn money."

There was a pause. Donna wondered what she should say. Had he called just to say hello to her, or was there a special reason?

As though he could hear her thoughts, Richard said, "I had a special reason for calling, Donna. But maybe it would be better if I discussed it with you in person. Is it too late for me to come over to your house for a minute?"

"Now?" Donna asked. What could be so urgent that it wouldn't wait until tomorrow? "Why, I guess that would be all right," she said.

"Gee, thanks," Richard said. "I promise I won't stay long."

Donna flew to comb her hair, and dab on a little fresh lipstick.

"Donna!" called Mr. Parker from downstairs. "How about giving your mother a hand with the dishes?"

Dishes! Goodness, was it only a little while ago that Uncle Roger had left? And now Richard was coming over. She had better tell her parents, and maybe they could be finished in the kitchen before he appeared. Wouldn't it be dreadful to have a "new" boy arrive when she was still drying pots and pans?

"You'll have to explain the whole thing again, Donna," Mrs. Parker said as she wiped finger marks off the refrigerator. "You mean that the boy who was leading the band at your dance just came over and talked to you at intermission time?"

Mr. Parker winked at his daughter. "I always told you this dark-haired beauty of ours stands out in a crowd, Grace. Shows that this Richard Whosis has good taste."

"Oh, Daddy," Donna remonstrated. "I wish you and Mother would listen. I just told you that I met him last summer while I was counselor at Camp Cherrydale. He was a counselor at Three Pines just a few miles away, and he and a friend of his asked Ricky and me to come to a square dance at their camp."

"But you haven't seen him since the end of the summer, have you?" asked Mrs. Parker. "And he remembered you all that time?"

"Of course he remembered me, Mommy. After all, I remembered him, didn't I? And he just graduated from Summerfield Junior High last year. He told me that the reason he hadn't called before was that he was so busy with senior high school, and his band."

"Sounds like an ambitious boy," said Mr. Parker, putting the evening newspaper under his arm. "Well, I'll just sit in the living room and carefully inspect him from behind my newspaper."

"Daddy!" called Donna after him. "Don't you dare!" Why did she have a father who was such a tease?

Then she stopped short. Would she prefer a father like Mr. West? "Poor Ricky," she thought sadly.

"Come in, come in," she heard her father say a few minutes later. "Donna's been waiting for you."

What a thing to say! Why hadn't she heard the doorbell ring?

Donna sauntered into the hall. "Oh, hello, Richard," she said. Was her father going to stand there forever?

"Sam!" came Mrs. Parker's voice from upstairs. "Could you come here for a minute?"

Thank goodness for mothers, Donna thought. Turning to Richard, she said, "Won't you come in?"

The boy ran his hand over his blond, slightly wavy hair. "Well, for a second, Donna." He sat down gingerly on the edge of the sofa in the living room.

Donna seated herself at the opposite end of the sofa. There was a moment's silence.

"Have you been having a nice vacation?" Donna asked brightly.

"Uh—oh, yes—sort of." Richard seemed fascinated by his shoes.

Again there was silence. "Goodness," thought Donna. "Why did he come here, if he didn't want to talk to me?"

Each question she asked seemed to lead to a dead end. Richard answered with a few words, and then Donna had to search for a new topic. It was apparent that the boy's mind was not on what she was saying.

Finally he looked at his watch and heaved a sigh. "I guess I'd better go, Donna. It's getting late." He stood up, and Donna led him to the front door, still puzzled by the conversation. Why in the world had he wanted to come tonight?

With his hand on the doorknob, Richard suddenly turned to her. "Someone gave me these today," he said in a rush of words, holding out four pieces of cardboard.

"They're passes for the movies, and they're good for any night this week. I thought maybe I could get another boy, and you and your friend could come with us—you know, that red-haired girl, Ricky, who was with you at camp last summer. I thought maybe we could go tomorrow night."

Donna tried not to let her excitement show. So this was what he had not had the courage to say before. "I'll have to ask my parents," she said, "but I'd love to go. And I'm sure Ricky would too. Oh—I just remembered, Richard. Ricky's mother is sick, and she has to stay home and take care of her. Could we make it for the next night?"

"Sure," Richard answered. "In fact, that'll be even better, because it will give me more time to get another boy. Gee, that'll be swell, Donna." He shook her hand warmly and rushed out the front door, almost tripping over the doorstep.

"It's not definite yet," Donna called after him. "It depends on what our parents say." But to herself she thought, "They'll have to say Yes. Oh, I hope Daddy liked him."

She ran upstairs, where her parents were finally putting suitcases away.

"Mommy, that was Richard!" Her father made a face.

"Now wait a minute, until I tell you what it was that he wanted."

"Well, maybe if Ricky will go with you," Mrs. Parker said, after Donna had told them about the invitation. "Frankly, I'm not too happy about children going to the movies in the evening without an adult."

"Children!" Donna almost screeched. Yeeks, what did her mother think she was, a five-year-old in kindergarten?

Mr. Parker gently nudged his wife. "Grace, how can you say such a thing? Of course she's an adult—well, almost."

Mrs. Parker, however, remained unconvinced. "Let's wait and see about Ricky," was all she would say.

The next morning Donna awakened with a feeling of anticipation. Something about today was different. She stretched and yawned, and then watched her curtains blow gently in the breeze.

"For one thing," she thought, "it's a beautiful spring day, and that alone always makes me feel good. And then Mommy and Daddy are home. And while I loved being on my own while they were gone, it's awfully nice to have them home again."

She wiggled her toes under the blankets, then leaned

on one elbow and looked out of her window at the backs of the neighboring houses. "And then there's Uncle Roger and the trip to California. Ooh, I can hardly wait till June. I've just got to get all *A*'s. I've got to!"

Then she sat up quickly. "And Richard! I almost forgot. Oh, I hope Ricky can come to the movies. Goodness, I promised I'd go over and help her today. At least that will give me a chance to talk to her about the date tomorrow. I wonder how she got along with her father. I'll bet it wasn't nearly as bad as she thought it would be." Then she thought of Mr. West, and was not so sure.

"If I straighten my room and the kitchen, then may I go to Ricky's, Mommy?" Donna asked as she carried her breakfast dishes to the sink.

Mrs. Parker nodded. "And Jimmy's room too, dear. I simply must polish some of this silver."

"Oh, Mommy. Not Jimmy's too. Why couldn't he do it himself?"

Mrs. Parker put a bottle of metal polish on the counter. "He asked for special permission to leave early this morning, dear. I think he said that one of the teachers had promised to help him with his baseball if he got to the park early. Something or other about control—you know I don't know a thing about baseball, but it sounded terribly important to Jimmy."

"Well, just this once," Donna sighed. "But never again. And I refuse to hang up any of the clothes he throws all over the room. After all, I have important things to do too." Doing Jimmy's room was sure to delay her another fifteen minutes, and she did so much want to talk to Ricky.

She rang the West doorbell impatiently. Goodness, she had rushed like crazy so she could get over here to help Ricky, and Ricky didn't even answer the doorbell. Could she possibly still be sleeping?

She shook her head. Ricky was such a dreamer. She didn't know a thing about running a house, about cleaning or cooking or anything like that. Donna had to admit that much as she disliked having to do these things, it certainly was helpful to know how in an emergency.

Well, if she were going to help, so that the Wests would give their permission for Ricky to go to the movies tomorrow night, she had better get started.

Finally she turned the handle of the front door. At least it wasn't locked.

She tiptoed into the large, old-fashioned living room.

"Ricky?" she called softly. Maybe she was upstairs. Or had Mrs. West gotten better, and gone out with Ricky? Certainly they wouldn't have left the front door unlocked.

Donna tiptoed over to the stairs, and called "Ricky?" There was no answer.

She looked around. The silence was almost unnatural.

"Ricky?" she called once more, a little louder. But the sound seemed hollow. Donna shivered slightly. What had happened to everyone? The place was as gloomy as a tomb.

Then, as she hesitated, wondering whether to go up to Ricky's room, her eye was caught by something moving in the upstairs hall.

As she gripped the heavy mahogany railing, a figure appeared at the top of the stairs—a figure dressed all in white.

CHAPTER 4   *Troubles Begin*

Donna knew immediately that the person at the top of the stairs was a complete stranger to her. But she was so startled that it took a moment for her to realize that the white clothing was a nurse's uniform.

"Can I help you?" asked the short, stockily built, middle-aged woman at the top of the stairs, with what Donna thought was a slight Scottish accent.

The dark-haired girl moved down a step. Something was terribly wrong, if there was a nurse here. Was Mrs. West worse? Or had something happened to Ricky?

"I—I'm a friend of Ricky West's," she said hesitantly. "Is—is she here?"

The nurse came down toward Donna for several steps, and leaned forward.

"She's sleeping," she announced in a loud whisper. "And

I didn't hear the doorbell, being with Mrs. West. The poor little lamb was up most of the night, she was that worried about her mother. So I thought the best thing was just to let her sleep this morning."

"I'm awake now, Miss Fairclough," said a voice at the top of the stairs. Donna looked up to see her friend, red hair tousled and one eye still not quite opened.

"I didn't know, Rick," Donna said softly. "I thought I'd help you with the housework, but I guess I'd better go."

"Oh, no," Ricky pleaded. "Please stay with me." Then she turned to the nurse. "How is Mother this morning?"

"She's resting comfortably right now," answered Miss Fairclough. "Now don't you worry your head about it, lambie. We're doing all that can be done for your mother."

Donna followed Ricky into her room, anxious to ask a dozen questions, but afraid to upset Ricky.

"Was dinner with your father all right last night?" she asked finally.

Ricky looked at her blankly. "Dinner?" Then she shrugged her shoulders. "I don't think anybody even ate dinner last night. By the time Father got home, Mother was much worse, and we had to call the doctor again."

"What did he say, Rick? Did he tell you what's wrong?"

"Oh, we knew that the night before, but the doctor didn't know how bad it would be. I guess I never told you that when Mother was a little girl she had rheumatic fever. I don't know exactly what that is, but I know that once you've had it, you can keep getting attacks, and it very often affects your heart."

Was Mrs. West's illness as serious as it sounded?

"Mother hasn't had an attack for a long time—not since I was a baby," Ricky continued. "Oh, Donna, you don't know how awful it is when your own mother is sick, and all you can do is sit and wait to see what happens."

"What does the doctor say?" Donna asked.

Ricky picked up a bottle of nail polish and began painting her toenails. Donna wondered if this activity was merely so Ricky could avoid looking at her; she had never seen her paint her toenails before.

"What does he say?" Donna repeated.

"Last night he wanted to take Mother to the hospital, that's what!" Ricky blurted out. Then she hid her face in her hands. "Oh, Donna, I don't want her to go to the hospital."

Donna went over and stood beside the chair, looking down at the still-uncombed red hair. She did not know whether a pat on the shoulder would comfort Ricky or make things worse.

"Well, she didn't go, Ricky, so maybe he thinks she's getting better."

"You don't understand, Donna." A tear-stained face looked up at her. "Mother simply hates hospitals—I mean, they really make her sick, even if she just goes to visit someone there. So finally Dr. Simmons said that he'd let her stay home if we could get a nurse. But he'll be here again this morning, and he told Father that if she isn't any better she'll simply have to go, whether she likes it or not."

Ricky squinted intently at the five bright pink toenails. "Anyhow, I don't want to talk about it any more. Tell me what you've been doing."

Donna twisted a lock of hair around her finger. "Well, gee, let me think . . . ." She couldn't possibly tell Ricky about the date for the movies, and make her feel worse. In fact, she didn't feel so very much like going to the movies herself. Poor Mrs. West!

Then she snapped her fingers. "Ooh, Ricky, how could I have forgotten? Remember when I called you yesterday? Well, my Uncle Roger had just come to visit us, and—"

"You mean your Uncle Roger who married Miss Fischer,

the teacher from our school?" Ricky's face brightened. "Was she there too? Tell me how she looked."

"No, she wasn't there. But something exciting happened."

Ricky listened, her eyes sparkling, while Donna told about the trip to California.

"And all you have to do is get good marks?" Ricky asked. "Oh, you'll get all *A*'s without any trouble, Don." Then her eyes took on that dreamy, faraway look that Donna had come to recognize.

"But that isn't all you'll get, Don," she said. "Ooh, I can just see the rest of it."

"See what?" Donna asked, in an exasperated tone. "What do I get with all *A*'s—a brass band, or a paper medal?"

"You're getting warm. Not a medal—an award."

Donna looked at her friend blankly.

"Don't you see?" Ricky explained in the tone of a patient parent teaching her small child. "Suppose you get all *A*'s, which you will if you put your mind to it. That's Scholarship. Then you also work on the school paper, and you're a representative on the Student Council, and you're on committees, and all that. That's Leadership. Now see?"

"Scholarship—and Leadership," Donna repeated thoughtfully. "Why, that's what you need to win the Outstanding Girl award when you graduate."

Ricky nodded. "Of course. Oh, Donna, wouldn't that be wonderful? Then there wouldn't be a doubt in the world about your going to California, would there? Your Uncle Roger said you had to get all *A*'s, didn't he? But your father said you'd just be mooning around. Well, that'll show 'em."

She squeezed the hand of her dark-haired friend. "Wouldn't it be terrific if you won the Outstanding Girl award, Donna? It's quite an honor, you know. And just think of the face on that stuck-up Joyce Davenport when your name is announced!"

"She's not really stuck-up, Ricky," Donna protested. "She's shy with people, and it's hard for her to make friends. But when people get to know her, they find out how nice she really is. And she's a lot brighter than I am. Why, I think she's always gotten *A*'s on her report."

Ricky screwed the cap on the bottle of nail polish. "That's just it, Donna! She may have Scholarship, but she doesn't have Leadership. The only reason she became editor of the school newspaper was because her father owns the *Summerfield Daily Bulletin,* and she worked there last summer, so she was the only one who knew anything about running a newspaper. Goodness, she couldn't get

elected Wastebasket Emptier, even if there was such a position."

Donna giggled. Then she looked at her friend thoughtfully. "Well, there must be lots of other girls who are more outstanding than I am. There's—there's—Anne Franklin, and"—she suddenly pointed at Ricky—"there's *you!*"

"*Me!*" Ricky snorted. "Do you think I care one eeny-weeny bit about those old awards? Not that I'd ever get one. But I'd never even try. All I want—" and her tone became wistful—"is for my mother to get well fast."

She yanked a comb through her tangled hair, and Donna followed her into the bathroom while she washed.

"No, Don," she repeated through a mouthful of toothpaste, "you're the one who has to get the award."

Donna looked at her own teeth in the mirror above Ricky's head. That bottom tooth was much more crooked than it used to be. Would she need braces?

"Do you think I really have a chance?" she asked, still inspecting the tooth.

"A chance? Why, you're *in*. And don't even tell your mother and father you're working for it. Let it be a surprise to them on graduation night."

Suppose Ricky were right? It really would be marvelous

if she got the award. She could just see her parents' faces. Maybe they would let her spend all summer in California.

Wasn't it wonderful to have a friend like Ricky, who was so loyal and had such confidence in her? Donna had no way of knowing that things would happen before graduation that would completely change her feelings toward her friend.

This warm Saturday morning, however, she smiled to herself. Ricky was right. She would do it! She would work harder than she had ever worked in her life, even if it meant staying up till midnight studying, and doing loads of extra reports and charts and things that teachers always seemed to like. By golly, she would win that award!

But just as she was turning to Ricky to tell her of her decision, the doorbell rang.

"Yeeks! That must be the doctor, and I'm not even dressed. Would you mind answering it, Don? Miss Fairclough keeps the door to Mother's room closed, so she can't hear the bell."

Donna nodded. "And then I'd better go home."

"Oh, no!" Ricky clung to her friend's arm. "Don't go yet. Wait until after Dr. Simmons leaves."

"Well, if you want me to," Donna agreed, realizing that

Ricky was upset, wondering what the doctor's decision about her mother would be.

Both girls sat quietly in Ricky's room, trying to catch the doctor's words, but all that could be heard from the front bedroom was the murmur of voices.

They both jumped when Miss Fairclough called Ricky's name softly from the hall.

"What is it?" the girl asked. "What did the doctor say?"

"Well, now," Miss Fairclough said, "Dr. Simmons would like to have a few words with your father, lambie. Do you happen to have the telephone number of Mr. West's office?"

"Oh, of course. But what did Dr. Simmons *say?*" Ricky grasped the nurse's arm.

Dr. Simmons came out of Mrs. West's room and went over to Ricky.

"Your mother has agreed that she would be more comfortable in the hospital, Ricky," said the doctor, keeping his voice low. "We'll be able to give her much better care there. I'm going to call your father now, and then I'll call an ambulance."

"An ambulance!" Donna never had seen Ricky's face so white. "Is she that sick?"

Miss Fairclough put an arm around her shoulders. "I'll

be going with her, lambie. There's nothing to be frightened of. It will just be an easier ride for your mother than having to disturb her to get dressed."

Ricky merely pulled at the fringe of her bathrobe cord, and looked from the nurse to the doctor.

"I'll stay here with you until your father comes home," Donna whispered, as Dr. Simmons went to the phone.

"Mr. West will probably want to go right to the hospital, lambie," said Miss Fairclough, frowning. "And I don't like the idea of leaving you here. Would you want to come with us in the ambulance?"

Ricky nodded. "I'll get dressed right away."

Donna rushed to help with her clothes, half listening for the distant sound of sirens. Then she realized that the bell probably sounded only when there was a patient being rushed to the hospital.

In a very short time the big, capable stretcher-bearers had carried Mrs. West down the stairs, and Ricky had been cheered considerably when her mother waved to her, and even tried to joke.

Donna stood on the sidewalk and watched while the ambulance drove off, with Ricky sitting in front with the driver. Then she walked home, hardly seeing the way.

The warm sun, the children playing, the people driving by on their own errands, all seemed a mockery. How could things be happening just as they always did, when Ricky and her mother were going to the hospital? It wasn't right.

"Well, finally!" Mrs. Parker said when Donna walked into the kitchen. "I thought you were only going over to Ricky's for a while, and you've been gone all morning."

"Oh, Mommy!" Donna said. "Please don't scold. You don't know what happened."

"I'm terribly sorry to hear it," Mrs. Parker said when Donna had told her about Ricky's mother. Then, trying to cheer up her daughter, "But after all, she may only be there a few days. I'm sure everything will be fine."

Donna looked at a note by the phone. "Is this for me?" she asked.

"I knew I'd forget if I didn't write it down," sighed Mrs. Parker. "Yes, it's for you. Richard White called. He wanted to know whether you had asked Ricky about the date for tomorrow. I said you'd call him in the morning."

"Gee, I couldn't very well ask Ricky, Mommy, with her mother so sick. Maybe someone else could go."

By the next morning, however, Donna had given up hope of getting someone in Ricky's place. The girls were either away visiting friends or relatives, or had baby-sitting jobs or had colds, or could not get permission to go.

"I never heard so many excuses in my life," Donna sighed by noon. "There simply isn't anyone left to ask. I guess I'll have to call Richard and tell him I can't go either. Maybe he can go with the other boy he's asked."

"Gee, Donna, I'm sorry about Ricky," Richard said when she called him. "But maybe it's just as well, because I couldn't get another boy. Do you think—I mean, would your parents—would they let you go with me, only the two of us? We could go to the early show."

"I'd love to, Richard," Donna replied. Wouldn't it be wonderful to have a real date with an older boy? "But I don't think they'd let me." How could she tell Richard that her mother didn't even want her to *double* date at night?

"Could you ask?" Richard insisted. "I'll call back."

"Please, Mommy," Donna begged. "If we leave at half past seven, we can be back by ten o'clock. If Daddy says it's all right, can I go?" She noticed signs of her mother weakening. "I'll call him at the office right now."

And if he hadn't finally said Yes, Donna was to think on graduation night, look at the sleepless nights she would have saved herself.

CHAPTER 5   *Not Really Richard*

"Oh, thank you, Mommy, thank you," Donna said, giving her mother a quick hug. "I promise we'll be back by ten o'clock. I'll call Richard right away."

On her way over to the telephone, however, she wheeled around and faced Mrs. Parker, a look of distress on her face. "But what'll I wear?"

Mrs. Parker put her hands on her hips. "Whatever I say will be the wrong thing, Donna. If I told you to wear your blue skirt, you'd want to wear your gray one."

Donna's face brightened. "May I wear my good gray cashmere sweater, Mommy, the one I got for Christmas? I know I promised to wear it only on special occasions, but I think a date is special, don't you?"

Mrs. Parker sighed. "I think it's a little warm for a spring evening, but if it will make you happy, I suppose it's all right. And which skirt will you wear with it?"

"Skirt? Why, my plaid Bermudas, of course."

"I should say not!" Mrs. Parker announced, in a very definite tone. "Personally, I think it's disgraceful the way you girls wear shorts to parties. But I certainly will not have a daughter of mine appear in public, in the evening, and with a boy, wearing shorts. Why, to me the most exciting part of a date used to be the dressing up."

"Oh, Mommy." Donna's disapproval was obvious. "In your day people did a lot of things they don't do today. You told me that Grandma didn't have her hair cut until after she was married. Does that mean that I should wear my hair in a big knot, with those huge hairpins dripping out?"

"Now, Donna—" Mrs. Parker warned.

"I don't care," the dark-haired girl pouted. "Everybody wears shorts, and I don't see why I can't, just because I have a mother who's so old-fashioned."

"It's not necessary for me to give any reasons," Mrs. Parker said coldly. "However, my own feeling is that half the trouble with the young people today starts with the way they dress. How often do you see a boy with a white shirt and a tie? Or a girl in anything but pants? I say it's a disgrace."

Donna continued to sulk. "Mr. Greer won't let us wear dungarees to school, and he makes the boys put their shirts inside their trousers, in case you're interested. But I can't see that it makes any difference. In fact, the one day we're allowed to dress in play clothes—on Blue Jean Day—is the day that's the most fun."

"School is not supposed to be merely for fun," Mrs. Parker said sharply. "And you, my girl, will either wear a skirt, or you will stay home tonight."

As Donna dragged into the hall and up the stairs, the front door banged shut. Quickly she whirled around.

"Oh, it's only you," she muttered, seeing that the newcomer was her brother.

"Whatsa matter with you?" he asked, but Donna did not deign to answer, and proceeded up the steps.

"What's eatin' her?" he asked, taking a handful of cookies from the jar on the kitchen counter.

"Nothing," sighed Mrs. Parker. "Donna has a date to go to the movies with Richard White, and she doesn't know what to wear!"

"Date?" Jimmy hooted. "You mean some guy is goin' to take old sour puss to the movies? Ha! That's a laugh. Well, there shouldn't be any problem about what she should wear. Just give her a broom, and she can go as a witch. Oh boy, that's a good one!"

Jimmy doubled over, holding his stomach with laughter. Suddenly he looked up, and found his sister glaring at him, and holding a large book which seemed ready to descend on his head.

The laughter stopped abruptly. "Mom!" he yelped. "Donna's gonna hit me!"

"Oh, I was not," Donna said wearily. "I brought the book down to show Mother. Only you'd better stop the stupid jokes; they're not funny."

"Please, please!" Mrs. Parker covered her ears with her hands. "Jimmy, go and wash your face. Donna, what did you want to show me?"

Donna pointed to the title of the book. "It's that book on teen-age manners, Mommy. If this says I can wear shorts to the movies, then will it be all right?"

"Donna, you heard what I said," Mrs. Parker repeated. "If the book agrees with me, fine. If it doesn't, that's just too bad. You either wear a skirt, or you stay home."

This time Donna almost flew to her room. She slammed the door. Why did she have to have such an unreasonable mother? Why couldn't she dress like everyone else?

Anyhow, she thought as she shoved her clothes along the pole in her closet, she simply didn't have anything to wear. The gray skirt with the gray sweater was too dead-looking. And the blue skirt was too long, and it had a spot on the front.

Why did her mother have to order her around and treat her like a baby? Wouldn't her parents ever learn that she was grown up? She simply would *not* wear a skirt.

She sighed. She did want to go to the movies tonight, and she would never be allowed to leave the house in shorts.

Then she snapped her fingers. Eureka! There was only one choice left. If that's the way they wanted it, she wouldn't wear shorts—or a skirt either. She would wear a dress! That would show them.

Delighted with her strategy, she began pulling things out of drawers. With her striped shirtwaist dress, she could wear her black flats and carry her new black patent handbag.

She was completely dressed after dinner that night, but still trying to get one lock of hair to lie flat, when Jimmy came bounding up the steps.

"He's here," he yelled. "Donna, that guy's here to take

you to the movies. And boy, is he all dressed up."

"Ssh!" Donna hissed. "Will you stop that yelling?" She pulled him into her room.

"What do you mean, all dressed up?" she whispered. "What's he wearing?"

"Oh, you know," Jimmy shrugged. "A shirt and tie like Dad wears to the office, and a fancy jacket. Gee, what some guys'll go through for a dame! How's he gonna sit through a whole movie when he's chokin' to death?"

Donna smiled. Wasn't it lucky she had worn this dress? She ran to open her top drawer, and grabbed her short white gloves. Then slowly, majestically, she walked down the stairs.

Richard was perched on the edge of the sofa, but he stood up when she walked into the room.

She extended her arm, and gravely they shook hands. "How nice you look!" she said graciously.

A warm pink color spread from Richard's collar to his hairline. "Uh—you do too, Donna."

Donna turned to her parents, who had come in from the dining room.

"I believe I'll just carry my short coat tonight, Mother," she said sweetly. "And don't bother waiting up for us."

"Oh, Donna," Richard said, "I promised your father that we'd be back by ten o'clock. Is that all right?" he asked anxiously.

"Anything you say," Donna answered airily, trying to act as though the ten o'clock curfew was Richard's idea, and not her parents'.

"Here, I'll carry your coat," Richard offered after they had said their good-bys and closed the front door behind them.

"Thank you," Donna murmured. *Golly,* she thought, *he really is a gentleman.*

She noticed that he was very careful to walk on the street side, and to help her up and down curbs.

What a change from those kids in ninth grade, she kept thinking. *Half the time the boys walk together and leave the girls all alone. Now* this *feels like a real date!*

"Uh—it's a lovely night, isn't it?" Richard was saying.

"Rather warm for this time of year," Donna replied. Goodness, how stilted that sounded. She looked at the sky. "The weather man says we'll have several more days of nice weather."

Why was she talking about the weather so much? Couldn't she carry on a simple, natural conversation? She

didn't seem to have a thought in her head.

"Are you enjoying senior high?" she asked after a few moments of silence, broken only by the sound of their heels on the sidewalk. School seemed to be a safe subject.

To her surprise, Richard looked uncomfortable. "Yes— I guess so. It's a lot different from junior high."

"Really?" Donna asked politely. "In what way?"

Again Richard looked uncomfortable. "Well, of course the work is harder, and there's a lot more homework. I sort of expected all that, though. It's just . . . ."

Donna waited for him to finish the sentence. Was he having trouble with his studies? She never should have started talking about school.

"Oh, here's the theater," Richard changed the subject, with obvious relief. "It's supposed to be a very funny picture. I hope you like it."

Donna waited while Richard exchanged his passes for tickets, then walked ahead while he presented them to the doorman, as she had seen her mother do.

"Where would you like to sit?" he whispered. Donna looked at him in amazement. Goodness, most of the boys just ran down the aisle, and the girls followed. Richard certainly was polite.

It *was* a funny movie. "Why tonight?" Donna thought in dismay, turning her head slightly away from the screen, and hoping Richard would not notice.

She had started to giggle right at the beginning, when everyone was quiet. Didn't anyone else in the audience think it was funny? Quickly she tried to stifle the giggle.

Then there was the part where the detectives were chasing the hero through those crowds of people, and getting into all sorts of silly situations. Everyone had laughed at that part, but her laughter seemed loudest of all. Really, she was making quite a spectacle of herself.

And now this. She kept stuffing her handkerchief in her mouth and trying not to look at some of the movie. But the whole thing was so hysterically funny, she thought she'd roll right off her seat. What would Richard think of her? He was such a gentleman, so polite, and here she was acting so ridiculous. Surely a lady would have better control of herself.

She took a deep breath, and straightened up. She simply had to make a better impression.

When the lights came on, she stood up. It had been a wonderful movie, but thank goodness it was over.

"It's only nine thirty," Richard said as they came out of

the theater. "I think we have time for a soda if you'd care to have one."

Donna nodded. Wait'll Jimmy learned that Richard had taken her out afterwards. Would her brother ever become so polite, so courteous? She shook her head. He could never be anything but an annoying little brother!

"This is delicious," Donna said as she sipped her chocolate soda. "And I enjoyed the movie, too, Ricky."

Richard looked up, and Donna blushed.

"Richard, I mean. I don't know why I called you Ricky, except that that's the name of my best friend. And your names are a great deal alike, you know."

"Richard—Ricky," the boy smiled. "They are a lot alike. People sometimes call me Dick, but never Ricky."

"If I called you Ricky, no one would ever know which one I'm talking about," Donna said. "I guess I'll just have to learn to keep 'Richard' and 'Ricky' apart."

The blond boy leaned forward. "It's funny you should say that, Donna. Should I tell you something that I don't think I've ever told a soul?"

Donna tried not to look surprised. What did he mean?

Richard put down the spoon which he had been holding, and carefully wiped a spot on the table with his paper napkin. "My name really isn't Richard."

Donna looked at him in amazement.

"Well, not my first name. Richard is my middle name."

"Oh!" Donna thought she understood. "I know. Sometimes mothers give their children queer first names, like Marmaduke or Agamemnon."

"Almost, but not exactly. You see my first name is Paul."

"Paul?" Donna repeated. "But that's a very nice name. I once knew a French count whose name was Paul. Why don't you like it?"

"Oh, I do. What I didn't like was my nickname. My mother used to call me Paulie. That was bad enough. But then the bigger boys began to call me Polly. Of course I hated that. So when we moved to Summerfield five years ago, I changed the order of my names and put the Richard first instead of second."

Donna laughed. "I don't think anyone would call you Polly today," she said admiringly, looking at his broad shoulders and comparing his height with most of the other boys she knew. Why, he was almost as big as her father.

"Of course Richard is a nice name too," she said as they walked home. "But I know I'd have trouble with you and Ricky." She half turned to her escort. "Would you," she asked hesitantly, "would you mind if I called you Paul?"

There was a silence which made Donna's heart contract. Had she said something terrible?

"I don't mind," the boy said finally. "In fact, I think it would be very nice if you called me—Paul."

Donna fidgeted. "Ninth grade is fun!" she stated loudly. "I'll hate to leave junior high."

The boy beside her took a deep breath. "Yes, it was fun for me too," he said. "Gee, I can still remember graduation night, and how excited I was when Mr. Greer announced that I had won the Outstanding Boy award."

"You *did?* How wonderful!" Should she tell him that she was going to try to win the girl's award this year? No, she had decided to keep it a secret, hadn't she, so if she did lose, nobody but Ricky would be the wiser.

"That's for scholarship and leadership, isn't it?" she went on. "Oh, I remember. You were president of your class, weren't you, Rich—I mean Paul? Tell me, did you get all *A*'s on your report?"

"All the time, Donna. Schoolwork has never been any problem for me. Just lucky, I guess."

Just smart, Donna thought to herself. Gee, some people had everything—good looks, popularity, and brains, too.

"I had a wonderful time in ninth grade," he went on. "Tenth grade is exciting, too, but I wish I knew what to do."

"About what?" Donna asked.

The boy shrugged. "It's a long, complicated story, Donna. It would only bore you."

"Oh, no," Donna said with feeling. "It wouldn't bore me at all. Oh, here we are, home already, Paul."

"I've enjoyed the evening a lot, Donna. Thanks for coming with me. Do you think I could see you again soon?"

"Won't you come in?" Donna asked. The walk home had been much too short. "Or we can sit out here."

Paul shook his head. "Thanks, but I'd better get home."

"But— but—" Donna called after him as he started down the steps, "aren't you going to tell me what's bothering you? I know it wouldn't bore me at all."

The boy paused and turned toward her. "Gee, Donna, I'd love to. Maybe you could help me. I've worried so much, I can't think straight any more. But"—he shook his head sadly—"I don't want to get you involved in it."

He turned away for an instant, then turned back to her. "Maybe some day I can tell you all about it. Some day when it's all straightened out. If it ever does get straightened out," he finished darkly.

CHAPTER 6   *Ricky Goes Wild*

"I thought I heard someone out here," said a man's voice behind Donna.

"Oh, Daddy!" Donna put her hand up to her heart. "Gee, you scared me. I didn't even hear the front door open."

"You did look as though you were up somewhere among the stars. But now that you're back among us mortals, how about coming into the house?"

Mr. Parker stepped aside to let Donna in. "You'd better report to Mother," he said. "She's been pacing the floor all evening, worrying about her baby. Now, *I* know you're quite a young lady"—he looked admiringly at his daughter—"but that idea hasn't quite penetrated your female parent's head yet."

Donna nodded in agreement as she hung her jacket in

the hall closet. "She certainly shouldn't worry about me when I'm with *Richard,* of all people."

Mr. Parker raised his eyebrows. "Really?"

"Is that you, Donna?" Mrs. Parker called from upstairs. "I'm in bed, reading."

Donna ran lightly up the steps. "Ooh, Mommy," she said, "I had the most scrumptious time. And Richard is such a gentleman. He could really teach Jimmy so much about manners."

Again Mr. Parker's eyebrows shot up. "And your poor doddering old father can teach him nothing, I suppose?"

"Oh, Daddy, you know what I mean," Donna protested. "It's just that Richard is someone Jimmy can look up to"—oh, dear, what was she saying—"that is, someone who's closer to his own age. And do you know," she rushed on, determined not to get more entangled in her own words, "his name really isn't Richard!"

"Ah-ha!" Mr. Parker puffed on his pipe, and blew out a cloud of smoke. "The plot thickens. Mrs. Parker, my dear, were you aware that we had entrusted the good reputation—nay, the very life—of our only daughter to the care of one who doesn't even use his right name?"

"Oh, Daddy!" What a time for her father to get silly,

and begin to talk like someone in an old-fashioned mystery. "If you'll only give me a chance, I'll explain."

"So Richard is really Paul," Mrs. Parker said at the end of Donna's explanation.

"Or is Paul really Richard?" Mr. Parker asked in a serious tone, pointing the stem of his pipe at his wife.

Mrs. Parker took off her glasses and laid them on top of her book on the night table.

"Sam," she said sternly, "this is no time for one of your Sherlock Holmes roles. If you're not concerned about your daughter's welfare, kindly leave us women to talk between ourselves."

"Well!" said Mr. Parker huffily. "I guess I know when I'm not wanted." And pretending to be very much hurt, he went downstairs.

"Your father may *think* he thinks you're grown up," explained Mrs. Parker, "but it's really just a joke to him that you're old enough to go out with boys." Then she settled back among her pillows. "Now tell me everything that happened."

Well, almost everything that happened, Donna thought. It would sound funny to tell her mother that Richard—or Paul—seemed terribly upset about something.

But even though she carefully avoided any mention to her mother of Paul's problem, her own thoughts kept going back to it. What could it be?

"And did he say anything about another date?" Mrs. Parker asked at the end of Donna's recital.

"Oh, Mother." Donna's tone was most disapproving. "You can't *rush* these things. He did ask if he could see me again some time." Goodness, first her mother wouldn't let her go out at all, and now she seemed dissatisfied that she didn't have more dates. Some people certainly were difficult to please!

"I almost forgot," Mrs. Parker said as Donna started to leave. "While you were gone, Ricky called. She seemed quite upset."

Donna stopped short. Ricky! In the excitement of preparing for the date and the fun of the evening, she had completely forgotten about Ricky. What a terrible friend she was. Here she had just had such a wonderful time, and Ricky had probably spent the evening at home all alone, or else with her stiff, unfriendly father.

"Is it too late to call now?"

Mrs. Parker looked at her bedside clock and nodded. "It's after ten thirty. And past your bedtime too, young lady. Now on your way. I expect your lights out in ten minutes."

Donna still dawdled at the doorway. "But didn't she even leave a message, Mommy? Didn't she even tell you how her mother was feeling?"

"Not a word, Donna. I said you'd call her first thing in the morning."

"What a long time to wait," Donna thought in her darkened bedroom a little later. She watched the moonlight, shining through the treetops, making patterns on her ceiling. "Thank goodness I don't have Ricky's problems. Or Paul's either—whatever they are. I wonder whether Paul will ever tell me what the trouble is. Let's see—it started when I said something about school."

Donna counted on her fingers. "It had something to do with school, but" —touching the next finger— "he said it wasn't about marks." Maybe by the simple process of deduction she could figure out what it was. She could play Sherlock Holmes just as well as her father, only she wasn't being silly about it.

She closed her eyes so that the patterns dancing on the ceiling would not distract her. "Now the third point," she began—and when she opened her eyes the sun was shining.

It took Donna a minute or so to realize that the night had passed. "I'd be a fine detective," she thought in disgust. "I'd probably go to sleep right in the middle of solving a fascinating case."

"Donna, are you awake?" Mrs. Parker called from the bottom of the stairs. "Ricky has called twice already."

Ricky! Quickly she pulled her bathrobe around her and ran barefoot down the steps.

"No shoes?" Mrs. Parker said. Donna knew what was coming.

"Just for one second, Mommy, while I call Ricky," she begged. "Then I'll go right back upstairs and get dressed."

Mrs. Parker sighed. "I really should be firmer with you."

"Hello, Rick?" Donna listened anxiously, to determine from Ricky's opening tone whether the news was to be good or bad.

Not good, certainly, she thought in despair when Ricky answered.

"I thought you'd never call, Donna," Ricky said in a dull voice. "She's—she's worse. They won't even let me see her. In fact, my father won't even let me stay at the hospital. He says it's too depressing, and that I'm better off at home."

"Maybe he's right," Donna said, trying to console her friend.

"But *he's* there," Ricky said accusingly. "He sits right outside Mother's room, so at least he knows what's going on. Oh, Donna, it's so terrible to be here all alone, and not even know what's happening."

Donna nodded, trying to find the right words. Then she put her hand over the mouthpiece of the phone, and whispered to her mother, "Mrs. West is worse, Mommy, and Ricky can't see her. May she spend the day here?"

"Of course," agreed Mrs. Parker. "Perhaps she'd like to bring a few things with her and stay overnight."

"That's a good idea," Donna said solemnly. But when she suggested the idea to Ricky, the red-haired girl refused.

"I want to stay close to the phone," Ricky explained. "My father said he'd call and tell me what the doctor said. And anyhow he wouldn't know where I am, and he'd worry. But, Donna"—the girl hesitated—"maybe you could come over here."

"Of course," Donna agreed. "As soon as I get dressed and have breakfast, I'll be right over."

Whatever do I say to her? Donna thought as she walked up the steps of the West house. She could picture the two of them spending the morning sitting like two little old ladies on stiff chairs, their backs straight, feet uncrossed, hands in their laps, now and then murmuring a word of comfort to each other. She sighed. After all, Ricky was her best friend, and surely she could do this much for her.

But to her surprise, Ricky opened the door with a whoop. "Hi-ya, Donna old girl. Gee, I thought you'd never get here. Wait'll I show you the new dance step I just made up."

Donna's jaw dropped. She closed her mouth quickly, hoping Ricky hadn't noticed. Sure enough, music was blaring from the record player in the living room.

"Come on, slow poke," Ricky urged. "Get your coat off and let me show you." She flung her arms wildly about, and kicked her legs in time to the music.

It was—why, it was disgraceful, Donna thought, shocked almost beyond speech. Mrs. West was so sick, and here was Ricky carrying on like a wild Indian.

"Now you do it, Don," Ricky urged. "See, it's easy." Then she stopped, almost in the middle of a kick. "Say, I thought of something better. Did you ever play 'Steal the Pack?' It's a baby card game, but if you play it real fast, it's loads of fun. I'll get the cards."

Donna sighed. What could she do? Ricky certainly was

a strange girl. Indeed, an hour later Donna was still aghast. Ricky went so quickly from the card game, which had been played with a great deal of shrieking and hilarity, back to the loudest records she could find. Then she dragged Donna upstairs to her mother's bedroom.

"Look at all this wonderful make-up!" she cried, opening the top drawer of the old-fashioned dressing table. "I've always wanted to try some of this stuff, and now's our chance." She began taking out eye shadow, mascara, eyebrow pencils, and all sorts of little boxes and jars.

"Of course Mother never uses any of this. Most of it is samples, or gifts. Ooh, look, Don—here's some gold nail polish."

"I'll just watch," Donna said. How would Ricky ever get all that junk off her face? The one time she had tried to use mascara, it had gotten into her eyes and stung like anything.

"Don't I look simply divine?" Ricky paraded in front of the dressing-table mirror, her face plastered with make-up. "Come on, Don. You try some too. It's lots of fun."

But just as Donna reached reluctantly for a bright red lipstick, Ricky sank down on the vanity bench. "Gee, I guess I'd better get some of this junk off before somebody sees me. Now where's that big jar of cold cream?"

She slathered the cream on her face and wiped it off carelessly with huge wads of tissue, leaving uneven streaks of color on her face.

"Now let's go get something to eat. I'm starved!" And before Donna could put down the lipstick she was holding, the other girl was down the stairs.

Donna shook her head. "I guess I'd better clean up some of this mess," she thought, picking up the pile of tissues and throwing them in the wastebasket. Whatever had gotten into Ricky? She had known her a long time, but she had never known her to act quite so dizzy. No one would ever believe that her mother was critically ill in the hospital. Wouldn't you think that she would be a teeny bit worried about her, and show a little concern? Instead, here she was acting positively giddy, jumping and running from one thing to another as though there weren't another thought in her head, as though—

Donna stopped, a box of powder in her hand. She put the box slowly in the drawer, and then hit her forehead hard. How stupid could she be! Of course Ricky was acting this way. She was simply trying hard, desperately hard, frantically hard, to push all thoughts of the hospital and her mother out of her head. Of course she had been laughing and screaming; why, she was nearly hysterical.

Donna sniffed, and realized that her cheeks were wet. Hastily she wiped the tears away. Now that she knew the explanation, how could she face Ricky? And Ricky would know she had been crying.

"Soup's on," Ricky called as she heard Donna's footsteps on the stairs. "Come on, kiddo. Hurry up before I eat everything in sight. I'm starved!"

"That's okay," Donna called, grabbing her coat from a chair in the living room. "I've got to run. See you later, Ricky." She slammed the door, and raced down the street.

"Hey, wait a minute," Ricky called after her.

Donna waved, and continued running until she had turned the corner. Then she stopped, and leaned against a mailbox to catch her breath.

"Poor Ricky!" she sobbed. "Poor Ricky!" She repeated the refrain all the way home, pausing every now and then to rub the mistiness from her eyes.

Without even stopping to hang up her coat, she ran to her room and buried her face in the pillow.

"Donna?" Mrs. Parker asked gently, coming over to the bed. "Is anything wrong?"

"It's about Ricky," Donna said mournfully, reaching for a tissue and blowing her nose. "I thought she'd be quiet, and sad, and unhappy. But Mommy, she's just the opposite, and, oh"—she blew her nose again— "that's a whole lot worse. Mommy, I simply couldn't stand seeing her trying to be so gay. I ran out of there so fast, when I realized what was happening." She swallowed hard and looked at her mother. "But I'm ashamed of myself. If Ricky can take it, why can't I? I'll never be able to face her again."

"It's too bad," Mrs. Parker said sympathetically. "I feel awfully sorry for Ricky, too. But as for not being able to face her—well, you might have a good reason for calling her right now."

Donna frowned. "I don't understand."

Mrs. Parker handed a white envelope to her daughter. "This came in the mail for you while you were gone."

Donna turned the envelope over. "It's from Dr. Duval," she said wonderingly. "Now what could he want?"

"Summer is a'coming in," Mrs. Parker reminded her. "And he probably has written to everyone who was a counselor at his camp last summer, to ask whether they want to come back this year."

"To Cherrydale? Ooh, Mommy, do you really think he

wants me to come back there again?"

"As your brother says, why don't you open it and see?"

Donna blinked and ran her eyes rapidly down the typed lines. Then she nodded. "That's just what it says," she reported. "Dr. Duval wants to know whether I'd like to be a junior counselor again this summer. How did you ever guess?"

Then she looked at her mother suspiciously. "You didn't open my mail, did you?"

"Donna!" Then Mrs. Parker smiled. "It didn't take much mind reading to figure it out."

"I guess not," Donna agreed. "Ooh, I wonder whether Ricky was asked, too. I'll have to call right away. Oh!"

"Now what?" asked Mrs. Parker.

"Why, that's what you meant about having a good reason for calling Ricky. I'll ask her about Cherrydale."

Mrs. Parker merely smiled. "What would we do without telephones?" she sighed.

What would we do without telephones? Donna thought, as she listened to the ringing at the other end of the line.

"Ricky doesn't answer," Donna said wonderingly, as she placed the receiver back on the hook. "But I just left her a few minutes ago. What is that girl into now?"

CHAPTER 7   *Another Date*

Every few minutes Donna tried to call Ricky on the telephone. "I wonder if she's at home, and just doesn't want to answer," she mused. Then she shook her head. "No, she said the reason she wanted to stay home was so that she could answer the telephone. Oh dear, I wonder what's happened."

When the doorbell rang, Donna jumped. "Let me answer it, Mommy," she called. "Maybe Ricky changed her mind about coming here after all."

But to her surprise, the doorbell-ringer was Paul. "Hi, Donna," he said, thrusting his hands in his pockets. "Can I come in for just a second?"

"Gee, I didn't think it was you, Paul," said Donna. "I —I didn't think I'd see you so soon." What a silly thing to say! It sounded as though she was annoyed by his coming, when really, except for the fact that she was worried about Ricky, she was very glad he had stopped by.

"I just wanted to ask you a question," the boy explained. "Could you come to a baseball game with me tonight?"

Donna clapped a hand over her open mouth. "A baseball game? Tonight?" she repeated in a dazed voice. Here she was, so worried about Ricky and her mother, but it didn't stop the rest of the world from going right on.

Paul shifted his weight from one foot to the other. "I know it's awfully short notice. It's a major league exhibition game, and of course Summerfield isn't big enough to have a team of its own, so we don't have much chance to see really first-rate baseball except on television, and tickets have been awfully hard to get, but I managed to get two passes at the newspaper office where I work, and it should be awfully exciting." He paused, completely out of breath.

"Oh, I don't mind the short notice," Donna said candidly. There really wasn't very much she could do to help Ricky, although she was so anxious to know what had happened to her. And it really would be nice to have another date with Paul. It was quite flattering to be asked out two nights in a row. But—baseball? Goodness, she couldn't even stand Jimmy talking about the game. How would she ever sit through a whole evening of it? Still, whenever she had passed the Summerfield stadium when something was going on at night, and the big arc lights lit up the sky for literally miles around, it had all seemed very exciting.

She felt that she had been standing in front of Paul for ages, but the thoughts had crossed her mind in seconds.

"I'll ask my mother," she said. "You wait here."

She was back in a very short time. "Mommy said I could go." She smiled. "I guess she was so surprised when I told her I wanted to go to a baseball game that she said Yes without thinking."

"That'll be swell, Donna. You don't mind taking the bus, do you?"

She had probably enjoyed the bus ride more than she would enjoy the game, Donna thought wryly, as they pushed their way through the crowds that evening.

Well, in a way it was her own fault for coming to the game in the first place. She never should have left until she was able to reach Ricky on the telephone. Of course, she had tried and tried all afternoon, to no avail. And she had asked her mother to keep trying while she was gone.

She sighed, following Paul up the steps which made an

aisle in the grandstand. There really wasn't very much she wanted to say to Ricky. Finding out whether she too had received a letter from Dr. Duval was only an excuse to call, and, in a way, an apology for running off that morning. Her main reason, actually, was to make certain that Ricky was all right; she had been acting so queerly, and the unanswered phone was very strange.

"Just stay close behind me," Paul said, turning to see that she was still following. "Our seats are right over there."

Donna nodded, and kept her eyes on the back of Paul's head, so she would not lose him. Some people were pushing her from behind, and she had to keep stepping aside to let the vendors by—men selling programs, and soft drinks, and hot dogs, and souvenirs.

"Everyone looks so happy," she thought. "I wish I could get into the spirit too." Then she shrugged her shoulders. It was silly to spoil her evening, and Paul's too. She was probably worrying for nothing. Most likely Ricky's father had called and told her that Mrs. West was better now, and she had gone to the hospital to see her. What a simple explanation that would be!

"Well, here we are at last!" Paul said with obvious satisfaction. "Gee, right by first base. Aren't these wonderful seats? I'm usually way out in the outfield someplace."

Donna nodded gaily. She was resolved to forget about everything but having a good time.

Why hadn't she listened to Jimmy during his long conversations at the dinner table? she thought as she watched the game. Terms like *knuckle ball* and *southpaw* and *double play* had always sounded like a foreign language— a language she had never bothered to learn.

"If I knew what was happening to the ball, I guess it would be more interesting," she thought several times. But it was such a little ball, and they kept throwing it to so many different people, that she could never follow it.

"Gee, it's exciting, isn't it?" Paul said as they got up for the seventh-inning stretch. Donna nodded, and smiled to show that she was enjoying herself. How could anyone be so enthusiastic about a ball game?

The last two innings seemed to go on forever. At the end of the ninth inning, with the score tied, Paul told her that the game would probably go into extra innings. So when a man named Capalbo made a home run which gave his team the extra run to win, and everyone went wild, she was delighted too.

"At least we can go home now," she thought happily.

Everyone was jumping up and down, and throwing papers into the air. She felt a sudden thump on her head, and turned to look at the people behind her.

A man with a rolled-up program turned red. "Sorry, miss," he spluttered. "I didn't mean to hit you."

"Oh, that's all right," she said gaily. Now that the game was over, she felt much better.

"Gee, I knew you'd like it, Donna," Paul said as they went down the steps. "It's so nice to go with a girl who doesn't ask a lot of silly questions."

Donna bent her head demurely, and followed Paul out of the stadium.

They waited with a huge crowd at the bus stop, and were jostled and shoved on board. Conversation was impossible in the noisy bus, and when they alighted a few blocks from Donna's house, the quiet in the darkened streets was startling.

Donna took a deep breath, to rid herself of the smell of popcorn and hot dogs and people. "Mmm," she sighed. "You can really tell it's spring, even though the trees are still bare."

"Yep," Paul agreed, strolling along beside her. "Pretty soon summer will be here."

"That reminds me!" Donna snapped her fingers. "You'll never guess who sent me a letter today. Do you remember Dr. Duval?"

Paul picked a twig from a hedge as they passed, "That short man with the little mustache, who was the head of the camp you went to last summer? Sure, I remember him. After all, our Camp Three Pines was only a couple of miles away. What did he want, Donna?"

"Oh, he just wanted to know whether I'd be willing to come back to Camp Cherrydale as a junior counselor again. And I don't know what to say."

She explained about her uncle's offer of a trip to California, and how she had to get all *A*'s in order to go. She even was tempted again to tell Paul about trying to win the Outstanding Girl award, then decided against it.

"But," she continued, "suppose I tell Dr. Duval I can't go to Cherrydale this summer, and then I don't get the trip to California either."

"Gee," Paul mused. "That's a tough one." They crossed the street, and he moved to her other side to be next to the curb. "Well, that's one problem I don't have to face. There's no chance of my going back to Three Pines."

"Oh?" Donna detected Paul's change of mood.

"I just hope Mr. Davenport will let me work longer hours on the newspaper. I've simply got to make more money." He spoke almost to himself.

"You did say you were working on the newspaper, didn't you, Paul? Isn't that how you got the tickets for tonight's game?"

Paul nodded. "Mr. Davenport has been awfully nice to me. Say—" He turned and looked at Donna with new interest. "His daughter is in your class, isn't she?"

"Joyce? Yes, and she's editor of our school newspaper. She learned a lot working on her father's paper."

"Gee, Donna." Paul's tone was wistful. "If you're a friend of hers, maybe you could put in a good word—" He stopped, and shook his head. "No, that wouldn't be fair." He seemed lost in thought.

Donna was afraid to interrupt. They walked along in silence for a moment. "Do you want to work there full time this summer, Paul? Maybe I could just mention it to Joyce, if I ever get the chance."

The boy looked at Donna thoughtfully. "I don't mean only during the summer, Donna. I mean right now!"

"Now? But we're going back to school in a few days, when spring vacation is over."

"Maybe you are," he answered glumly. "But—well—gee, Donna, I think I'll quit school and go right to work."

Donna gasped. "Quit *school?* Oh, you couldn't, Paul!"

"Well, I'm not sure, Donna. And please don't mention a word of this to anyone. Promise?"

"I promise," she said solemnly. "Can you—could you—tell me why you want to quit?"

"Uh—here we are," Paul said. "Here's your house." He seemed loath to leave.

"We can sit on the front steps, if you'd like," Donna offered. "Daddy doesn't usually put the porch furniture outside until Memorial Day. But it's such a nice night I don't think we'll get cold."

The boy hesitated. "If you don't mind," he said after a moment. "I'd really like to tell you about it, Donna, because I'm sure you'd understand. And I've just got to have someone to talk to."

And he chose me, Donna thought with pride, as they settled themselves on the top step. Paul sat at the end, with his back against the railing.

"Can't you talk it over with your father?" she asked, trying to be helpful. Could a boy confide in his father the way she did in her mother?

"My father?" Paul snorted. "That's a good one. My father is the person who got us into all this."

"I don't understand."

Paul wriggled to a more comfortable position. "The reason I want to quit school is because my family needs the money to live on, and my father isn't making any."

"Oh, that's too bad," she said sympathetically.

"You don't have to feel sorry for him," the boy continued bitterly. "He had a perfectly good job, and he gave it up."

"Didn't he have any reason?" Donna asked gently.

"We-ell, yes," he admitted. "You see, he was a salesman, and he traveled a lot. He didn't like that too well, but there wasn't much he could do about it. Then his company was taken over by new management, and they wanted him to travel even more. If he had accepted, he would have been away almost all the time. Dad said he had little enough time with his family as it was."

"That sounds like a good reason to me."

"So far, yes. But then he decided that he couldn't look for another job while he was working for this company, so he just quit."

"And hasn't he been able to get another position since then?" Donna asked.

"Oh, sure," Paul answered, with a wave of his hand. "But none of them are good enough for him! For two months now he's been looking for a job, and not one that he's been offered has satisfied him."

Donna shivered slightly in the cool night air. She hoped Paul had not noticed.

"And the terrible part about it is—" He stopped.

"Yes?" What was it that Paul found so difficult to say?

"The awful part is—my *mother* had to go to work!"

Donna could see how upset the boy was. She could picture Paul's mother kneeling beside a pail of steaming sudsy water, her face flushed as she pushed some straggling hair away with a rough, reddened hand.

"I know how you must feel, Paul," she said sympathetically. "But I'm sure your mother is doing what she thinks is best for the family. There's nothing really wrong in her working, you know, though I guess it is hard on her."

Paul sighed. "And she's being so—so *brave* about it, Donna. She keeps saying that she's always wanted to go back to being an interior decorator."

"An interior decorator?" Donna repeated. "Is *that* the work your mother is doing?"

Paul nodded glumly. "She used to be one before she

was married. She keeps saying that she just loves to help people pick out furniture for their houses, and show them what color to paint their walls and all that stuff. And then she comes home and tells us all the troubles she's had all day—how the factories got the orders wrong, or how fussy her customers are. I'm sure she'd much rather be home."

He turned his head away, as though talking to himself. "Why does my father have to be so particular?" Then he slammed his fist into the palm of his hand. "How can he stand seeing my mother working when he's doing nothing! What kind of head of the house does he call himself? Doesn't he know that it's a man's job to support his family?"

Donna was startled by the outburst. "But, Paul," she protested, "why will your leaving school help? You still won't make enough to support your family. And I'm sure your father will get a job very soon, anyhow."

Paul sighed. "That's what my mother keeps saying. Oh, I know I won't be making very much. But at least I'll be paying my own expenses. At least *I* won't be a drain on the family finances." He turned to Donna, his expression grim. "You do understand, don't you, Donna?"

But, thought Donna, still rather shocked by the situation, *I can't say I agree with him. Surely there must be a better solution than leaving school."*

Aloud she said, "What do your parents say, Paul? Do they know that you want to go to work?"

Paul nodded. "My mother feels terrible about it, even though I've never actually told her my real reason for quitting—I couldn't hurt her that way. She's tried everything to get me to change my mind." He sighed. "That's one reason why I still haven't definitely decided what to do. On one hand, I know how much it means to her to have me graduate and go on to college. On the other hand, I hate to see her working and my father doing nothing."

"And how does your father feel?"

"Oh, him!" Paul dismissed him. "He's only too happy to have me leave, I think—although of course he's never really come out and said as much. He left school himself before he graduated, and he never even took any courses afterwards. All he says is that I'm sixteen now, and old enough to get working papers, so he guesses I'm old enough to make my own decisions."

"I suppose you could go to night school," Donna said frowning. "But it would take so long. Couldn't you earn almost as much money from your after-school and weekend work?" Maybe that was the answer. "After all, you

not only have the newspaper, you have your band, too—
the one that played at our school dance."

"That's not enough, Donna. I've got to do this right."

"You mean," Donna tried to phrase it as delicately as
possible, "you feel that if your father won't act like the—
the head of the house, you've got to do it for him?"

"Correct," Paul agreed vehemently.

"I—I don't know what to say," Donna said, still turning
the matter over in her mind. "I know how you feel, Paul,
really I do," she assured him. "It's just that I think it's so
important to get an education. For one thing, it'll be much
easier for you to get a good position later. You could make
a lot more money later on, don't you think? And there's
still so much we have to learn."

She felt that Paul was not even listening. "I'm sorry I'm
not much help," she apologized.

But then, she thought as she went inside after Paul had
left, *he wasn't much help to me in deciding what to do about
Camp Cherrydale, either. Of course, I will admit that Paul's
problem is a lot more serious than mine.*

Although she had no way of knowing it, by the very
next morning Donna was to feel that even Paul's problem
paled into insignificance beside the new events of the day.

CHAPTER 8 *A Nightmare*

She was running. She had been running so long that she was out of breath, but still she kept calling, "Wait for me!" She was almost sure that the girl in the distance was Ricky, and she simply had to catch up to her. If only she would turn around and wait for a moment. And then, just as she got close enough to be positive that it was Ricky, she found that she was running away from the red-haired girl.

"But I have to find her!" she wept. "Why did I run the wrong way?" She looked at the streets and houses around her, and realized she was lost. "And now I don't even know where I am," she thought, beginning to be afraid. "How shall I ever get home?"

At that moment Paul appeared, almost out of nowhere. "I'll help you get home," he said with a noble air. "Just stay with me."

But after they had walked and walked, she realized that Paul was lost too. He stopped suddenly, and scratched his head. "I don't know where to go," he admitted. Then, with his usual firmness, he added, "But we're certainly not going to stay here. We're going to go—*that* way."

He began to walk, seeming to expect her to follow him. "Oh, no," she started to cry out. "That's not the right way. I'm sure it's not!" But she did not know how to stop him.

They had walked only a few steps down the side street when they found themselves in a great arena. They were surrounded by people who were yelling and pushing, and though she tried desperately to stay with Paul, they were separated very quickly.

The people pushed harder, and forced her to move up the steep stairs. "Let me go, let me go," she shouted, but her voice was lost in the din. "I don't belong here. I didn't want to come. Please let me go."

But the men back of her were annoyed by her cries, and began to hit her on the shoulder with rolled-up programs. No matter where she tried to run, they were after her, hitting the same shoulder all the time.

Hitting—and shaking—and—hitting. . . .

She opened one eye. Mrs. Parker was still shaking her

gently by the shoulder. "Donna, get up. Donna, do you hear me?"

Donna sighed deeply, and shuddered. "Ooh, Mommy, I just had the most awful dream. I guess it was a combination of everything—Paul and Ricky and the baseball game —but I was so scared."

"It didn't seem to make you sleep any less soundly," Mrs. Parker commented. "You'd better get up now. Ricky's on the telephone."

"Tell her I'll call back, Mommy." Donna yawned, and snuggled under the blankets. Then she looked up. "Where was she all yesterday afternoon? And for that matter, you couldn't even reach her last night, could you? Gee, I'll bet while we were so worried about her she was out having a good time, someplace or other."

"I—I don't think so," Mrs. Parker merely stated. "And I don't think you'd better call back. She said she'd wait while I woke you, but she can't wait all day. Hurry down. Here are your bedroom slippers. Now go quickly."

Mrs. Parker's tone was urgent. Goodness, Donna thought, it wouldn't hurt Ricky to wait another minute. She really wasn't fully awake even now. What was so important? She would never have thought she could be so tired from merely watching a baseball game.

"Hello, Rick?" Donna said sleepily into the mouth-piece. "Wherever were you all yesterday?"

"Oh, Donna!" At Ricky's tone, Donna was shocked fully awake. There was an anguish in her friend's voice that she had never heard in anyone's before.

"Ricky!" Donna whispered. "Is—is your mother worse?" Sobs shook the phone.

"Ricky, what is it? What—what's the matter?"

"Oh, Donna," came the wail. "Oh, Donna, what'll I do?"

"I—I don't know what you mean." Donna's stomach turned over. She knew she was about to hear something terrible.

"Last n-night," the girl stammered, and then the words came out in a rush, "last night my mother died!"

All Donna's insides seemed to harden into a lump. Her head started to throb, and the telephone shook in her hand.

"Oh, no!" she breathed. "Oh, no!"

"At eight o'clock last night," Ricky sobbed.

Donna's throat was dry. "Oh, no!" she whispered. "Oh, Ricky!"

"C-Come over and s-stay with me, please. C-Could you?"

"Of course. Right away." Slowly Donna replaced the

receiver. It wasn't possible. It couldn't have happened. Not to her very best friend. This must be part of her dream.

But she knew it wasn't. While she and Paul had been at the game enjoying themselves, this had happened.

"Oh, Mommy!" she cried, running to the stairs. "Oh, Mommy, it's so awful!"

"I'm right here," Mrs. Parker said from the living room.

Donna turned and looked at her mother wide-eyed. "You knew, didn't you?"

Then she buried her head in the older woman's lap, and sobs shook her body.

How could it have happened? Everybody *had* to have a mother! Suppose it had been her own mother! Just by chance, it had been Ricky's. She sobbed harder.

"Now, Donna," Mrs. Parker smoothed her daughter's dark hair. "You know that Mrs. West had had a bad heart condition for a long time. She was very lucky to have been so well, and to have led such a normal life, all these years. Of course it's a terrible thing, and I know how hard it is for Ricky. We'll have to be extra specially nice to her."

Donna wiped her cheeks with a tissue from her bathrobe pocket. "I promised I'd go right over and stay with her, Mommy." She sniffed again. "But I'm afraid. What can I say to her? I won't know how to talk, or act."

"Just act naturally," Mrs. Parker assured her. "Try to talk about other things, if Ricky's interested. Otherwise simply listening to her will be a help. It's good to have someone to talk to at times like this."

Donna nodded. Whatever she could do to ease Ricky's pain, she would certainly be more than glad to do. First there had been Paul's problem about quitting school. Then she had had that terrifying nightmare. And now this. It was too much for her to bear.

Mrs. Parker looked at her daughter soberly. "Donna, life isn't always pleasant. There are a great many things that happen to us in this imperfect world that we simply have to learn to accept, no matter how unpleasant or tragic they are. And most people do learn to face them. Somehow, somewhere, inside ourselves we find the strength to go on. I'm sure Ricky will, too."

Donna sat quietly, listening to her mother's soothing voice. Usually she hated it when she had to listen to these little lectures—sermonizing, she called it—but somehow today it seemed to calm her.

"Now get dressed so you can go over to Ricky's."

Donna sighed. "Could I wear my dungarees, or should

I wear a dress?" This was all such a new experience.

"Certainly not dungarees. There will probably be other people at the West's, Donna—family and friends. Dress as you would to go to school."

Other people! That hadn't occurred to her. It would be hard enough to face Ricky, but a lot of strangers, too. . . .

To her immense relief, when she stepped into the West living room a little later, it was empty. Apparently it was still too early for people to begin to pay sympathy calls. Or maybe they hadn't heard the news yet.

"Fredericka!" Mr. West called up the stairs. "Donna Parker is here!" Then he turned to Donna. "If you'll excuse me," he said with his usual courtly manner.

"Hi, Donna," Ricky said as she came down the stairs. "I was just cleaning my room."

Except for the fact that her face was so pale that each freckle seemed to stand out by itself, Ricky looked very much as usual. The sobs that Donna had heard on the telephone seemed well under control.

"I think I could bear it more if she were weeping," Donna thought. "But this business of acting so gay yesterday, and hiding her feelings, is more than I can stand."

She wanted to put her arms around her friend, to hold

her close and soothe her, as her mother had done for her. But something in Ricky's manner warned her not to touch her, or to show any display of sympathy or affection.

"Do you mind coming into the kitchen, Donna? I haven't done the breakfast dishes yet."

Ricky led the way, then stopped at the doorway to the kitchen. There, at the sink, stood Mr. West, a small apron covering very little of his large frame.

"Oh, Father!" the red-haired girl cried in dismay. "You don't have to wash dishes. You never did before."

But her father merely smiled. "You know your job is to dry. Now you just pick up the dish towel, my dear, and you'll see what a good dishwasher I am."

Ricky hesitated. "I wish you'd let me wash, Father. Donna will help, won't you, Donna?"

The dark-haired girl nodded. It was obvious that Mr. West was trying very hard to be helpful, but she knew that he was not the type to do housework.

How would they ever manage? Who would do the cleaning and the cooking? Mrs. West had never insisted on Ricky helping with the housework, and Ricky had never had a desire to learn. Besides, school would be starting soon. She supposed they would have to hire a housekeeper.

"Ricky helps me with my work lots of times, Mr. West," Donna said. "I'd be glad to help her today. I'll dry, and she can put the things away." For Mr. West had continued to work at the sink.

"I can see that you ladies are much more efficient than I am," Mr. West said as he finished scouring the last pot, and placed it in the dish rack. "Frankly, I think I've had enough of being in the kitchen for one day. Thank goodness Aunt Alice has invited us there for lunch."

Ricky's face fell. As soon as Mr. West had left the room, she turned to Donna.

"Father is trying so hard to be nice to me," she said. "He called Aunt Alice first thing this morning, to ask if she would take me shopping. I need a new dress for the— the—" She refused to say the word. Then her face darkened. "But I hate Aunt Alice; she's so old-fashioned. She'll probably insist on buying me something that will make me feel like a freak. She treats me as though I were about six years old, and simple-minded at that. And children aren't supposed to have any opinions—they're supposed to do as they're told, and eat what's put before them, and all that. Oh, why did Father say we'd go there for lunch! It'll be bad enough just going shopping with her."

Ricky stopped as Mr. West wandered back into the kitchen. He seemed to have no idea of what to do next.

"Didn't your mother always do the dusting when she finished in the kitchen?" he asked hesitantly. "Where does she—did she—keep the dust cloth, Ricky?"

Ricky's voice seemed to catch in her throat. "We—we'll do the dusting, Father. Come on, Don. You take the cloth, and I'll take the sweeper and the mop."

She ran to get the things, and her father meandered out of the room again.

As Donna dusted the table in the front hall, her eye was caught by a familiar envelope, addressed to Ricky.

"Oh, Ricky!" she said delightedly. "You got a letter from Dr. Duval too."

Ricky peered at the envelope. "Gee, I almost forgot about it. Yes, he asked whether I want to go back to Cherrydale as a junior counselor, the way we did last year. Doesn't that seem ages and ages ago, Donna?"

"What have you decided, Rick? Will you go?"

Ricky looked at the envelope intently, as though expecting the answer to appear on it. "I don't know, Donna. I haven't even thought about it. Summer seems a million years away, and I can't make plans so far in advance."

Donna nodded understandingly. "Of course, Rick. He said we didn't have to let him know for a couple of weeks. In fact, I don't even know what I'm going to do. If I don't go to California, I think I'd want to go back to camp. We had to work hard, but it was fun, too. And at least it's better than staying home for the whole vacation."

Ricky scarcely seemed to have heard. "Come on, let's finish cleaning. Aunt Alice will be furious if we're late."

"There," she said a little while later. "That'll have to do, even if it isn't as good a job as my—as other people would have done," she finished lamely.

"I'd better go home now," Donna said, realizing that Ricky and her father would have to leave very soon. She had carefully avoided mention of her dates with Paul, though it had taken a great deal of self-control. Still, with Ricky looking so forlorn, it had not seemed right to discuss the good times she had been having.

"Thanks for coming over, Don." Ricky seemed reluctant to have her friend depart. "Do you think you can come back tomorrow? You can at least see the elegant dress my dear Aunt Alice has picked for me. Gee, I certainly don't look forward to this afternoon."

She looks so—so lost, Donna thought as she walked

home in the bright sunshine. *And the house is so empty. Ricky and her father seem to float around in it.*

After the depressing atmosphere at the West house, she was surprised to see children playing noisily outdoors. "Ssh," she wanted to say to them. "This is a very sad day. It isn't right to make all that noise."

When a car honked its horn, she wanted to silence it. She was shocked to hear a boy whistling a tune. "But they don't know," she had to remind herself. "For them, life is the same as it was yesterday."

Suddenly she stopped. Every single day tragedies occurred. Every day there were accidents, and deaths, and illnesses. You read about them in the newspapers, and somehow it didn't even touch you; it was merely a story. Only when it happened to you, or someone close to you, was it real.

Perhaps in a way, it was a good thing. Life had to go on. People couldn't stop living. It was fine that the sun was shining. She could see the buds beginning to burst on the hedges. Spring was a little late this year, but it was comforting to know that, no matter what happened, it would finally arrive in all its gaiety, with its promise of a new life.

"This is what it means to grow up," she thought. She felt infinitely older, and wiser, than she had the day before.

CHAPTER 9   *Rivals*

"Mommy, I think I ought to write to Uncle Roger and tell him I can't go to California," Donna said as she helped prepare dinner.

Mrs. Parker closed the refrigerator door and turned around. "Really? You've given up so quickly? Donna, I thought you had more staying power than that."

"Oh, it's not because of the marks, Mommy," Donna corrected her. "If I worked awfully hard, I'm sure I could get all *A*'s. No," she shook her head, "it's because of Ricky."

"Ricky?" Again Mrs. Parker's tone expressed surprise.

"If she goes back to Cherrydale, I think I ought to go back too, to be with her. She looked so awfully—well, lost, today. And after all, I am her best friend."

Mrs. Parker finished scraping a carrot. "That's very considerate of you, Donna. But perhaps you should see what Ricky's plans are first. Wait for a few days until she's ready to discuss it again. Sometimes it isn't wise to make a sacrifice without first making sure it's wanted."

As if she didn't know Ricky! Donna thought as she set the table. She had no idea how stunned she would be when she talked it over with her friend.

The opportunity came the very next day, when she went over to see Ricky's dress.

"Thank goodness Father came along," the red-haired girl said. "He may be stiff and formal, but he's the only one who can manage Aunt Alice. At least I was able to get something pretty, instead of the dreadful black with a high collar and long sleeves that she picked out for me."

Donna looked approvingly at the quiet but youthful dress hanging on the door of Ricky's closet. "Your father must have good taste," she said.

"Oh, he has," Ricky agreed. "I'm learning a lot about him, Donna. Of course, he isn't really fun, like your father, but I think that's because he's still shy with me."

Well, thought Donna, at least Ricky didn't seem nearly so scared of her father as she had a few days ago. Was it possible that she and her father would become friends?

"Do you know," Ricky was saying, "this was the first

time I ever went shopping with him? I thought it would be ghastly, but it wasn't at all. He knew just what to tell the salesgirls. It was very nice, going shopping with a man."

Apparently the afternoon had done Ricky a great deal of good. She was much less subdued than she had been the day before, and she seemed to have shed the "lost" look.

"And, oh, Donna, I forgot to tell you the best part!" Ricky hugged herself and twirled around. "Father has promised me a television set of my very own, to keep right here in my room. In fact, he's already ordered it, and it's a beauty. And he said he'd buy me new bedroom furniture too. I'm going to have the most elegant bedroom in all of Summerfield!"

"That's wonderful!" Donna exclaimed. Ricky looked so pleased—what a change from yesterday!

"And he's promised me a lot of other things too. He said as soon as the weather gets really warm, I can start taking riding lessons. I'm going down to Newman's store next week and have them measure me for a whole riding outfit."

Donna was a little taken aback. She had wanted to have riding lessons for years and years, and now it was Ricky who was going to have them.

Then she scolded herself severely. "Just remember why

Ricky's getting all this," she told herself. "Would you change places with her for one minute?" Still, Ricky was certainly getting a tremendous number of gifts from her father.

"Gee, that's great," she said aloud. "I'm sure it'll be loads of fun."

"And then there's one other thing that he told me. But you'll have to promise that you won't say a word to anyone because it's not definite yet," she said solemnly. "It's about this summer."

"Oh, have you decided?" Donna asked. "I told my mother last night that if you wanted to go to Cherrydale—"

"No, no," Ricky interrupted impatiently. "I wouldn't go back to that stupid old Cherrydale. Not when Father has promised me that I could have this yummy trip."

"A trip? Oh, Ricky, could you come to California with me? Ooh, that would be wonderful. I know Uncle Roger would be delighted to have you come, too. He told me that there's a special room for me, and I'm sure we could share it. We could go to visit the movie studios, and have lunch at the Brown Derby, and . . . and . . . ." Her voice trailed off as she looked at her friend's face.

"Have you finished?" Ricky asked disdainfully. "If

you'll keep still for a minute, maybe I'll get a chance to tell you the plan."

Donna gulped. "Go ahead."

"Well," Ricky said, hugging her knees, "last night Father was talking to me about school. I guess he was worried about my doing good work for the rest of the year. Anyhow, he told me how pleased he and Mother had always been with my report cards, and he hoped that nothing would change that. He said he realized that I was graduating soon, and he and Mother had decided to do something special for me as a graduation present, maybe a trip or something."

Ricky stared into space, a slight smile on her lips. "And then—I don't know what made me say it—I told him that I would like to do something as *my* graduation present to *him*. He looked sort of surprised, and honestly I didn't have the faintest idea what I was going to say next. But it popped right out—I told him that I'd like not only to get good marks, but that I wanted to be at the top of the class. I'm going to get all *A*'s, Donna!"

So Ricky would be trying for all *A*'s, too. Would she want them to study together?

"And my father was so pleased that he said that if I did

do well, he'd take me with him this summer on a trip to Europe—to England, and France, and Italy! He has to go on business, and he said if I did outstanding work, he thought I'd deserve the trip. Wouldn't that be simply dreamy?"

The red-haired girl lowered her voice. "And when he said that, do you know what I thought right away?"

Donna shook her head dumbly.

"If he does something so special for me, then I ought to do something more than just get good marks, Donna." She leaned toward her friend. "Father doesn't know it, but I've decided to try for the Outstanding Girl award!"

Donna's jaw dropped.

Was Ricky serious? She couldn't be! Why, that was what she, Donna Parker, was working for. In fact, it was Ricky herself who had suggested the idea. Didn't she realize that this would make them rivals? Didn't she care any more? Or had she simply decided that anything she wanted, by rights belonged to her?

"Donna!" Ricky said sharply. "You weren't even listening. Didn't you hear what I said? I'm going to go to Europe with my father this summer. And I'm going to win the Outstanding Girl award!"

CHAPTER 10   *An Invitation*

Donna tugged at her bureau drawer. "Nothing ever goes right for me," she muttered, and pulled again. "Why doesn't this stupid old drawer open?"

She hit the drawer hard with the side of her fist, to no avail. In desperation, she kicked at the chest. "This mean old bureau! I never liked it in the first place. I wish I could just throw it out and forget about it."

She kicked harder this time, then stamped her foot. "How am I supposed to get this miserable room cleaned up today, when I can't even open my drawers to put things away?" She addressed the drawer directly. "Now open you—you—" Words failed her, and all her energies went into pulling.

Apparently the extra wrench did the trick, for not only did the drawer come loose, but the impact made Donna stagger and drop it on her foot, spilling the contents all over the floor.

"Ow! Ow!" she yelped, holding on to her toes with one hand, and dancing around on the other foot.

"Good heavens!" said Mrs. Parker, rushing into the room. "What is all the commotion about?" Then she looked at Donna, the drawer, and the mess on the floor.

"Whatever has gotten into you, Donna? For the last few days you've been simply impossible. You just can't go around the house slamming and banging things about. I know you're upset about Ricky's mother, but—" She was interrupted by a loud ringing of the doorbell.

"I'll get it," Donna said quickly. Anything to get away from one of her mother's speeches. She was in no mood to be lectured.

"Why, Joyce," Donna said in surprise. "And Anne, and Mary, and Norma. Oh, hi, Karen, I didn't see you at first. Come in. What is this, a party?" It was so good to see some of the gang.

"Gee, no, nothing like that." Joyce answered for the group. "Come to think of it, this is the first spring vacation I can remember when there haven't been any parties, or outings, or anything."

"Life certainly has been dull," Karen added. She paused. "But there are some kinds of excitement we could do without."

The girls looked at each other. Then Anne spoke. "We just heard about Ricky's mother, Donna. I guess you knew already."

"Oh, yes." Donna nodded.

"Well, we sort of thought we should pay her a visit, and we'd like you to come with us."

"Now?" Donna asked, a little taken aback. She hadn't seen Ricky since the day she had learned about the trip to Europe. She hadn't spoken to her on the telephone, either, half expecting Ricky to call and ask for an explanation.

But Ricky hadn't seemed to notice her absence, which had hurt her feelings even more. She hadn't even invited Donna to attend the funeral. And although Donna had been relieved, at the same time she had felt rather let down at not being asked to play the role of best friend.

"No," she said. "You go without me."

There was a heavy silence.

"Well," said Joyce, "we'd like to have you, but I guess you know what's best. Are you sure that it's all right for us to go?"

"Quite sure. Ricky will be very glad to see you." *And brag to you, the way she bragged to me,* Donna thought angrily.

The girls chattered for a few minutes about the reopening of school the following Monday, and then left. Donna trudged back to her room.

The sight of the disheveled room was the last straw. She threw herself on her unmade bed, and buried her face in the pillow.

"Donna!" Mrs. Parker's voice made the unhappy girl look up. "What's the trouble now? Why did the girls come here, and then leave so quickly?"

"They only wanted me to go to Ricky's with them, Mommy."

"And you said No? Why, Donna? I've wondered why you haven't been going over there. Aren't you the girl who, not so long ago, was willing to give up a trip to California in order to spend the summer at camp with her best friend? Now you won't even go to visit her."

"Well, if I've changed, Mommy, she's changed a lot more. At first she seemed to want to be with me, but she's interested in other things now." She told her mother of Ricky's television set, and new clothes, and riding lessons.

"And it wasn't the fact that she got all those things that bothered me, Mommy. Goodness, I realize that her father is just trying to be nice to her. But it was the way she talked about them, as though those things made her better than anyone else. And—and then—" She stopped.

"And then what?" Mrs. Parker prodded, determined to learn the entire story.

Donna picked at a hangnail. Should she tell her mother that she and Ricky were rivals now? "Well, the other thing was that her father promised her a trip to Europe this summer. And do you know why?" She looked at her mother earnestly, then told her the whole story of the award. It was good to confide in someone at last.

"You see, it was Ricky's idea in the first place that I try to win, and now she's going to try to get it away from me. And I did so much want to surprise you on graduation night."

"Well!" Mrs. Parker sighed. "Really, Donna, I'm astonished at you."

"Astonished at *me*? Why?"

"First, because I see no reason for you to be angry at Ricky because she wants to win the award. There's no rule that says that only one of you can try for the prize, is there?

Isn't it your marks, and leadership, and general attitude, that determine who wins?"

Donna nodded glumly.

"Frankly," Mrs. Parker continued, "your father and I would be delighted to have you try to win the prize. And I'm sure Uncle Roger would be ever so pleased, too, simply knowing that his promise of a trip has made you want to work harder than ever."

Donna brightened. "He would, wouldn't he?"

Mrs. Parker did not return the smile. "But that certainly is no reason for Ricky not to consider herself a candidate, too. And I'm surprised that you should feel that way about it. Which brings me to the other point."

Donna said nothing, but looked down at her hands. Goodness, was there more?

"You'll never have a chance of winning, Donna, if you don't change your attitude. And that's what distresses me most of all."

Donna looked up, wide-eyed. "My attitude about what?"

"About Ricky. You show so little real sympathy for her. Don't you see that she's hanging on to material things, like clothes and furniture, because she doesn't know what else to hang on to?"

"You don't understand," Donna argued. "I just finished saying that I didn't mind her getting those things, or anything else she wants. But she doesn't have to be so awfully stuck-up about it, does she? Anyhow, it'll make her so spoiled that no one will like her. Wait'll you see," she prophesied darkly.

"You judge people much too harshly," Mrs. Parker replied. "Ricky is having a very difficult time now, whether you think so or not. Remember, Donna, we never know how we'd act in a strange or new situation until we're faced with it."

"I'd certainly never do something I'd have to be ashamed of," Donna answered hotly. "I'd certainly never forget that I'm just a plain ordinary girl from Summerfield Junior High School. And I'd never forget my best friends!"

Mrs. Parker only smiled, which made Donna angrier than ever.

"I hope you're right, dear. I hope that you always do remember those things!"

Donna had no idea how soon she was to be reminded of the conversation. "It didn't make much sense to me then," she was to say, "but I think I understand now!"

For the present, however, she only knew that her mother

was being extremely unsympathetic.

"Hey, you're wanted on the telephone, Donna," Jimmy called, clattering halfway up the stairs. "It's a bo-oy," he added in a singsong.

"You don't have to be so loud," Donna shushed him. "Didn't he give you his name?"

Jimmy shrugged. "Didn't ask him."

She certainly didn't get any co-operation in her own home, Donna thought snappishly. A mother who didn't understand her at all, and a brother who was noisy and wouldn't even take the trouble to answer the telephone properly.

"Hello," she said curtly. She wasn't at all in the mood for one of those long, silly, boy-girl conversations.

"Donna?" She recognized Paul's voice immediately, though she hadn't heard from him since the night of the baseball game when he had told her about quitting school. She had never seen a boy so concerned about making money.

"It seems I never give you very much notice. I hope you don't mind. But I wondered whether you'd like to go to the movies with me tonight."

And have to listen to more of his troubles, Donna thought

bitterly, as though she didn't have enough of her own.

"Oh?" she said coldly. "Did Mr. Davenport give you more passes?"

"Passes?" Paul asked wonderingly. "No, I don't have passes. But the picture is supposed to be good, and I thought you'd like to see it."

"You mean you'd spend your very own money on me?" she asked, her voice heavily sarcastic. "Oh, I couldn't let you do that."

"Wh-what do you mean?" the boy asked uncomfortably.

Donna didn't seem to be able to stop herself. "I thought money meant so much to you," she said. "I thought you couldn't even finish high school because you simply had to go out and make a lot of money. Well, if it's so important to you, I certainly wouldn't let you spend any on little old me."

"I—I'm sorry, Donna," Paul said in a low voice. "I never thought about it that way. Good-by."

"Wow!" Jimmy said. "I'll bet that's the last you see of that guy. He sure hung up fast. Who was it?"

"Paul," Donna answered dully. What had ever possessed her to talk to him like that?

"Paul!" her brother wailed. "The one decent guy who

ever came into this house! Gee, he was even gonna take me to a baseball game some day. Wouldn't ya know it? Girls just have no sense."

It was only because she had been angry at her mother, Donna thought. And that had been because of Ricky. Well, whatever the reason, it had been a miserable day, and she wished it would end. She had had enough things go wrong. In fact, she wished the whole vacation would end. How would she ever spend the time until Monday?

To her surprise, the remaining few days flew by, mainly because of a letter which arrived for her in the next morning's mail.

"It looks like one of those fancy formal invitations," she said thoughtfully, turning the large cream-colored envelope over in her hand.

"Oh, Mommy, it is!" she cried, scanning the delicate black lines on the folded sheet which she took out. "It's for me. An invitation to Bunny's wedding!"

Mrs. Parker came into the front hall, drying her hands on a kitchen towel. "Bunny? Bunny who?"

"Bunny Knight, Mommy. You remember—she was my senior counselor at Camp Cherrydale last summer. I knew she was engaged, but I didn't think she'd be getting married so soon. Imagine—she wants me to come to her wedding."

She looked at the invitation again. "Where is Nottingham, New York, I wonder? I remember Bunny saying that it isn't far from New York City, but I don't know how to get there. Oh, well, we could find it on the map."

Then she looked at her mother. "Do you suppose I ought to go, Mommy? After all, I wouldn't know anyone there but Bunny."

"Let me think about it," Mrs. Parker said, returning to the kitchen.

"Wait, Mommy, there's something else in the envelope." Donna drew out a small white sheet of paper. "It's a note from Bunny." She read avidly for a moment, then let out a little screech.

"Ooh, read it, read it, Mommy," she cried, handing her mother the note. She leaned her chin on the older woman's shoulder, so she could read it with her.

"She wants me to be a bridesmaid! Isn't that dreamy! Just think, me a real honest-to-goodness bridesmaid. Now I'll *have* to go to the wedding."

Mrs. Parker put the note down on the hall table. "Give me a chance to think about it, Donna. There's a lot involved, you know."

Donna followed her mother into the kitchen. "But Bunny says she's getting the gowns for the bridesmaids, Mommy. That's why I have to let her know right away, so she can get the correct size. Pink organdy sounds luscious, doesn't it?"

"Of course Bunny's buying the gown is a help," Mrs. Parker agreed. "And I suppose you have enough other clothes to take with you."

"Then what is it, Mommy?"

Mrs. Parker filled an empty ice tray with water, and put it back in the refrigerator. "For one thing, Donna, you have your final examinations about then, don't you?"

Donna looked stricken. "Oh, gee," she said in dismay, "I never thought of that." Then, with renewed purpose, she consulted the large calendar hanging above the sink.

"Let's see," she said, tracing the dates with her finger. "We finish our exams the day before Memorial Day, so we can practice for graduation the whole first week of June. Oh, Mommy, it works out just perfectly."

"It does? How do you figure that?"

"Don't you see? Bunny is getting married on May thirty-first, which is a Saturday. Our exams are over on May twenty-ninth, which is a Thursday. Memorial Day is on

Friday, so school is closed. And the gorgeous part is that I could leave first thing Friday morning, so I can have most of Friday at Bunny's house. You know she said in the note that she'd like me there the day before, in order to rehearse."

"Now hold on a moment," Mrs. Parker warned. "That arrangement sounds satisfactory, I'll admit, but—"

"Well, we said the clothes part is all right. And you agree that the dates are fine, and I'll be all finished with my tests. So what else can there be, Mommy?"

"It's a point you yourself brought up, Donna. After all, the only person you'll know there is Bunny. We're not acquainted with her family at all. I'm not sure that your father will approve. And what's more, I'm not sure you'll feel comfortable."

"You can convince Daddy," Donna pleaded. "I know you can. And Bunny said that I'd be sharing a room with her cousin, who's exactly my age. Oh, Mommy, it would be so exciting. I'm sure I won't feel at all uncomfortable. Bunny is like a big sister to me."

How could I ever have known what I'd be getting into? she was to muse afterwards. *And to think that I begged to be allowed to go!*

Mrs. Parker cast a glance in her daughter's direction.

It had been days since she had showed so much animation. If this would stop the moodiness, and the tantrums, maybe it would be a good idea.

"I guess I could call and talk to Bunny's mother," Mrs. Parker said. "You can usually tell a great deal about a person, even from a short telephone call."

Donna flung her arms around her mother's neck. "That would be wonderful, Mommy. And Daddy would be satisfied, too. Oh, that's a marvelous idea. Then you could tell her that I'm accepting the invitation."

"You'll have to write anyhow," Mrs. Parker said. "I can't accept for you."

Donna nodded solemnly. "I will. May I do it right now, Mommy? Is it settled?"

"It depends on the phone call. And on what your father says. And"—Mrs. Parker put up a warning finger— "on how you behave. If you expect to be treated like an adult, you'll have to act like one." Then she softened. "But I guess it's *almost* definite."

"So my little girl is going to be a bridesmaid," Mr. Parker said that evening, after a very satisfactory call had been made to the Knights in Nottingham. "Just be sure you don't catch the bride's bouquet, sweetie."

Donna dimpled. "The girl who catches it is supposed to get married in a year, isn't she?"

Mr. Parker nodded, a twinkle in his eye. "It's nice to have a glamour girl in the family, but it would be shocking to have a child bride. It wouldn't do, you know, for a man in my position."

Donna patted his hand. "Don't worry, Daddy. I'm sure I won't get married before I'm fifteen, or do anything else to shock you. I'm just a plain, ordinary girl."

The words re-echoed as she fell asleep. "A plain ordinary girl." When had she said that before? Suddenly she recalled. It had been while she was talking to her mother about Ricky. "I'd certainly never forget that I'm a plain ordinary girl from Summerfield Junior High School." No matter what happened, she thought as she fell asleep, she would remember that. She was to learn that events sometimes have a way of changing the firmest resolutions.

CHAPTER 11 *A Bowling Game*

"Mommy, may I go over to Joyce Davenport's house this afternoon? She just called and said that Anne Franklin and Karen were coming over, too. You know how much it means to her to feel that she has friends."

Mrs. Parker nodded. Joyce had been known as "The Brain" for years, and the girls had only recently discovered that she could be interesting as well as intelligent. "Anything special, dear?"

"No." Donna adjusted the buckle on her belt. Gracious, was she getting fat again? It was probably all this sitting around during vacation. She had better begin doing those waist exercises if she wanted to fit into the gown for Bunny's wedding. She couldn't wait till it arrived.

"Why don't you all take a ride on your bicycles, and get some fresh air?" Mrs. Parker suggested.

"Yeeks, Mommy. Girls my age don't go riding around town on bicycles. That's for children." But an afternoon of sitting and talking did sound boring. After all, she would see the girls in a few days anyhow, when school began.

"I know!" She snapped her fingers. "Let's go bowling."

"That's a wonderful idea," Joyce said when Donna called her. "I'll reserve an alley." Then she hesitated. "I—I don't play very well, Donna. I'm not much at sports, you know. Will Anne and Karen mind?"

Donna laughed. "They play as well as I do. I think the highest score I ever got was sixty-nine."

"It's a good thing the place is almost deserted," Anne said that afternoon, bending her lanky frame down to pick up a ball from the rack. "I'd be ashamed to let those teams that come here in the evening see us." She watched in disgust as her ball rolled halfway down the alley, then made a sharp turn to the left and continued in the gutter.

"And Joyce was worried about not playing well enough!" Donna laughed. "If any of us knocks down more than three pins at a time, it'll be a minor miracle."

"I once watched a man make seven strikes in a row," Karen said, her blue eyes shining. "And some day I'm going to do that, too."

"Ha!" said Anne. "I'd be happy to have one, just once in my life."

All the girls turned, as a group of boys walked in and stationed themselves at an alley at the opposite end of the hall.

"Aren't those some of the boys who played in the band at our spring dance?" Joyce whispered.

Donna wanted to look more carefully. Perhaps Paul was among them. She wondered whether he would speak to her, after the way she had talked to him on the telephone.

But at a glance none of the faces seemed familiar. She didn't know whether to be relieved or sorry.

"Don't look," she said. "They'll think we're trying to flirt with them. I'll just finish this frame and then we can go." Goodness, she wouldn't want those boys, whoever they were, to think she was interested in them.

Donna crossed her fingers, then picked up the ball, and aimed it carefully down the middle of the alley. There were still seven pins standing out of the ten.

Six pins went down with a crash, and the seventh wavered. "Ooh, make it fall down," she whispered. "Then it'll be a spare and I can have an extra turn." But the seventh pin somehow righted itself, and remained standing.

"Wow!" Anne said. "For a minute you had us scared. Too bad you didn't get a spare, but that was pretty good anyhow."

Donna looked up from the score sheet. "Oh, well, my total is seventy, so at least it isn't any worse than before."

The girls changed their shoes and left. "In a way I'm glad I didn't get the extra pin. Those boys were looking at us in such a funny way," Donna said. They walked toward the shopping district.

"Prim little Donna!" Anne laughed. "Maybe they were looking at us because we seemed sort of familiar to them, too." She wiped her forehead. "But I'm glad we stopped when we did. As far as I'm concerned, that's enough exercise for one day. How about a little refreshment at the Sweet Shop?"

Donna looked at the other girls. "Gee, I really shouldn't. I must have gained forty-eleven pounds this week, and if I don't watch out I'll never get into my gown!"

"Gown?" Anne, Karen, and Joyce all cried together.

"What gown?" Joyce added. "Are you going to a formal? Ooh, tell us all about it."

"No, it's not a formal," Donna answered. "And if I'm going to tell you about it, I may as well be comfortable.

But don't let me get any whipped cream in my soda."

The girls settled themselves in a booth, ordered, and leaned their elbows on the table.

"Well," Donna started slowly, "one morning an invitation came in the mail." She was enjoying the attention immensely.

"Oh, Donna," Joyce said disapprovingly. "That's not what we want to hear. Tell us the end first, and then go back to the beginning and give us the details. Otherwise we'll simply die of suspense."

"If that's the way you want it," Donna agreed. "I'm going to be a bridesmaid!"

The reaction could not have been more satisfactory.

Donna leaned back and waited for the gasps to subside. Then she proceeded to give the particulars—all about Bunny, and where they had met, and what kind of gown she would wear, and when the wedding would take place.

"Gee, aren't you so thrilled you can't *sleep?*" Karen asked. "What did Ricky say when you told her?"

Donna's smile faded. "As a matter of fact," she said with a toss of her head, "I haven't mentioned it to Ricky."

The arrival of the sodas interrupted an awkward pause.

"We were there a couple of days ago, you know," Joyce

said after a few moments. "To see Ricky, I mean. She was telling us about all the new things her father is buying her."

"In fact, that's all she could talk about," Karen added sourly. "And she showed us all the travel folders she's gotten about Europe. She said her father was going to take her there this summer. Is that true, Donna?"

"Gee, I don't know," Donna said. She had thought the trip was supposed to be kept secret, and here was Ricky practically broadcasting the fact. "Did she tell you why she was going?"

"Oh, just some story about her father promising to take her if she does well at school, and that she's trying to win the Outstanding Girl award at graduation to please him," Joyce said. "But she seems so sure of going that she's even picked out the boat that they're going to sail on."

"You know," Anne said thoughtfully, "I've always liked Ricky. She's usually such a sweet person, and nice, and fun to be with. And I felt awfully sorry for her when I heard about her mother."

Joyce and Karen nodded agreement as Anne spoke.

"But the other afternoon she was so—well, different. And even when I tried to be sorry for her, I couldn't."

Donna shredded her paper napkin. "I can understand

her wanting a lot of things right now." She remembered her mother's words, about Ricky needing something to hang on to. "And I wasn't going to say anything about the award, but since Ricky's already told you, I guess it won't do any harm."

"Is there something else?" Karen asked.

Donna repeated the conversation she had had with Ricky about her Uncle Roger's offer of a trip.

"All I said was that I wanted to get all *A*'s, so that I could go to California this summer," she said. "And it was completely Ricky's idea that I try for the award. Why, it had never occurred to me. But she kept insisting that I ought to win it."

She pushed the shreds of paper napkin into a pile. "I told Ricky that there were a lot of people who I thought were better qualified." She looked up. "Gee, Joyce, you always get all *A*'s." She quickly put out of her mind what Ricky had said about Joyce not being able to be elected Wastebasket Emptier.

"Oh, no!" Joyce said, shrinking into her corner of the booth. "It's taken me all this time to live down my reputation as a Brain. I wouldn't want to start that all over again," she finished, shuddering.

"I'd better rush," Donna said, rising quickly. "See you at school on Monday."

Only two more days of vacation. She hoped her father had some plans for the weekend, so the time wouldn't drag. Sometimes he would load the whole family into the car and just drive and they would see the most interesting places that way. She didn't want to spend the next two days in the house.

But it was her mother who presented an idea that took her completely aback.

"How would you like to spend your next-to-the-last day of vacation in New York?" Mrs. Parker asked after dinner. "Daddy and I thought that, since you haven't done very much this week, you might like the change."

Donna took a deep breath. "Oh, Mommy, are you serious? Do you mean it? Of course I'd love it! But what would we do? Would you and Daddy both come?"

"No," Mrs. Parker said, "in answer to your last question. I thought maybe we'd look for a wedding present for you to send to Bunny, if you'd like. And then maybe we could get tickets for the ballet."

She smiled at her husband, who had hidden his face behind the evening newspaper.

"And since neither of those activities would have any particular appeal for your father, perhaps he wouldn't object to our leaving him for this one day."

"Oh, don't mind me," Mr. Parker said, peering out from the paper. "But aren't you going to ask—"

"Never mind, Sam," Mrs. Parker said quickly.

What was going on? Did her mother have some other purpose in making the trip? It did seem awfully sudden.

Donna looked at her mother quizzically. "Then just you and I will go, Mommy? And Jimmy will stay home with Daddy?"

"Well, now," Mrs. Parker said brightly. "I thought maybe you'd like to ask Ricky to come with us. You haven't seen her for a while, and I'm sure the change would be good for her, too."

"Oh!" Donna glowered. So that was it! This was her mother's tactful little way of forcing her to make up with Ricky. She was about to refuse the invitation, when she suddenly reconsidered.

After all, why should she let Ricky keep her from an exciting time in New York? Then, too, maybe a day with her supposed best friend would convince her mother that she was right.

"If you want me to ask her, I don't care," she said in an offhand manner. "I guess I'd better call her right away."

Then she brightened. "It's awfully short notice. And we'll have to leave very early tomorrow morning if we want to get any shopping done. Maybe Ricky won't be able to come."

But Ricky seemed delighted at the invitation.

"Oh, that'll be simply wonderful, Donna," she said. "My father told me that the next time I went to New York I could look for a graduation dress. And you and your mother would be able to help me, wouldn't you?"

"If there's time," Donna replied. Of all things! Now she would have to spend the morning watching Ricky try on dresses.

Mrs. Parker, however, seemed delighted to be asked to shop with Ricky. "Poor little thing," she said. "She simply has no one to turn to."

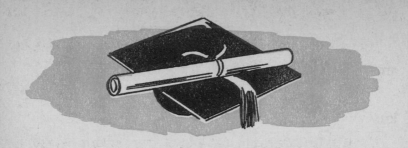

CHAPTER 12   *The Trip to New York*

"Let's walk, instead of taking the bus on Fifth Avenue," Donna said to her mother. "It's such a lovely day, and it's so much fun to be right in the crowds. Everyone hurries so in New York!"

"Do you mind walking, Ricky?" Mrs. Parker asked.

The red-haired girl shook her head. "Oh, not at all, Mrs. Parker. I'm anxious to see the shop windows, anyhow. I'll have to begin planning the wardrobe for my trip, you know."

Donna nudged her mother, but Mrs. Parker paid no attention.

"I'm so glad we made an early start," Donna said, her dark eyes sparkling, and drinking in the sights around her. "We have two whole hours before lunch. Have you decided where we're going to eat, Mommy?"

"No place special, Donna. We'll see how far along we are in the shopping. Where do you want to go first?"

"Well . . . ." Ricky hesitated. "I know exactly what kind of dress I want. I just hope I can find it someplace."

"And I haven't the faintest idea what to get Bunny for a wedding present," Donna said. "Isn't there a store where we could look for both things, Mommy?"

Mrs. Parker paused, as if to get her bearings. "There are several, but let's start at my favorite place. It's only a few blocks away, and they have a lovely gift shop too."

The gift shop was most impressive. "Especially the prices," Donna whispered, as she examined an ash tray with a tiny price tag on the bottom. "Imagine fifteen dollars for an ash tray!" she exclaimed. "This place is much too expensive, Mommy."

"Now just a minute." Mrs. Parker had to catch her daughter's arm as she started to leave the department. "I'm sure that there are things that cost less, too. Let's ask one of the saleswomen to help us."

"Why, I think we have just the thing," the woman said. "Especially since you're not sure of the kind of furniture the bride is going to have. You wait right here, and I'll bring it to you."

In a few moments she was back, carrying a large cardboard box. From out of the excelsior and papers within, she took a perfectly plain large glass bowl.

"How lovely!" Donna said. She was sure Bunny would like it.

"It's so simple, and yet it doesn't look ordinary," Ricky said. "And it would go with anything."

"And it could be used for so many things," Mrs. Parker commented. "As a salad bowl, or for fruit, or even to keep flowers in."

Donna beamed. Then her face fell. "How—how much is it?" she asked with a frown.

"That's the nicest part," the saleswoman said, smiling at her. "It's only five dollars."

"Including the gift wrapping?" Donna asked in astonishment.

"Including everything," was the answer. "And if you don't mind paying a few cents for postage, we'll even mail it for you."

Donna looked questioningly at her mother, who nodded.

"And can I put a gift card in it?"

"Right over there." The saleswoman put the bowl back into its wrappings.

"Well!" Donna heaved a sigh of relief. "That was quick, wasn't it? And I'm sure Bunny will like it."

"I'm glad too," Ricky said. "Now we'll have more time to shop for my dress."

Donna turned to reply, then caught her mother's eye and shrugged.

"Maybe we should have our lunch before the rush begins," Mrs. Parker suggested. "We could eat right here in the store."

Ricky looked crestfallen.

"Otherwise we might have to spend a lot of time waiting in line, and then we'd be late to the ballet," Mrs. Parker explained. "I promise we'll leave time to look for your dress, Ricky."

"Goodness, there's a line already," Donna said, as they came to a section of the store completely enclosed by glass. Over the doorway hung a sign with a coy girl fish, her long eyelashes fluttering, and the announcement that this was The Goldfish Bowl.

"Ooh, there are tanks of tropical fish all around," Donna pointed out as they walked past the entrance to take their place in line. "Aren't they beautiful?"

"But where are the tables?" Ricky asked. "All I see

are chairs like the movable ones we have at school, with those big arms for desks."

Mrs. Parker smiled. "You'll find out in a few minutes. Now aren't you glad we came early?"

"Why do we have to pay before we go in?" Donna asked, as they moved closer to the cashier, who was stationed at the head of the line.

"All the meals are the same price," Mrs. Parker explained. "You can get your choice of a salad bowl, or a sandwich platter, or a hot dish. And I think you'll like the desserts, too."

The girls followed Mrs. Parker, as a hostess led them to a group of three chairs facing one another. They watched open-mouthed as a pink-capped waitress set small wooden trays on the arms, each tray covered with a gaily patterned paper mat on which were set silver, a napkin, a coaster with an empty glass, and a menu.

In quick succession there appeared a girl to fill their water glasses, a girl to add little packages of sugar, salt and pepper to their trays, and still another to take their order.

"Gee, they certainly have a system," Donna said after they had all decided to order the salad bowls.

"What's the cart that the waitress over there is wheeling?" Ricky asked.

"Those are the desserts I was telling you about," Mrs. Parker explained.

"Can we choose anything we want?" Donna half rose from her chair to get a better view, then sank down. "Oh, why do desserts have to be fattening?"

The salad bowls, with tiny sandwiches arranged on top, were delicious, but the girls could not wait until the dessert cart was brought to them.

"Look at that magnificent coconut cake!" Donna crooned. "And deep-dish apple pie, and chocolate eclairs, and French pastry."

"If you really want to diet," Ricky said, "on the bottom shelf there's jello, and stewed fruit, and baked apples."

"While you girls are making up your minds, I think I'll take the strawberry chiffon pie," Mrs. Parker said.

The girls watched as the waitress carefully slid a generous-sized helping of the whipped-cream-covered pie onto a dessert plate. Inside there was a fluffy delicate pink filling.

"I guess I'll take that too," Ricky decided.

"Me too," Donna sighed. She tasted a mouthful of the

pie, and closed her eyes in rapture. "Maybe I'll have to stop eating for a few days, but it's worth it."

"Now, we still have a little while to shop for Ricky's gown before we have to pick up our ballet tickets," Mrs. Parker said, leading them out of The Goldfish Bowl.

"Wow! Look at the line now! Imagine waiting in that!" Ricky said.

"I'm awfully glad we had lunch first." Donna glanced sideways at Ricky, but the other girl did not seem to realize that the remark was meant for her.

"And here is your department, Ricky." Mrs. Parker stopped in front of a rack of white and pink gowns.

"Ooh, this one is lovely." Donna took out a hanger with a white net dress, the neckline slightly scooped and the skirt very full.

Ricky pushed it aside. "Oh, no, that's not at all what I had in mind."

A saleswoman in a sleek black dress, her hair pulled tightly back in a bun, came over to them.

"I may help you?" she asked politely, with a slight accent.

"I want a graduation dress," Ricky explained. "But nothing like that." She waved at the dress which Donna still held against herself as she looked into the mirror.

"Then perhaps zees one?" the woman asked, taking out a white cotton which had a square neck, and rows and rows of lace sewed around its wide skirt.

"Oh, isn't that simply divine!" Donna squealed. "If I didn't have that white dress with the little rosebuds that Uncle Roger gave me for my birthday. . . ." she looked at her mother.

"Absolutely not," Mrs. Parker said firmly. "Ricky is looking for a dress, Donna, not you."

"Anyhow, I don't like it," Ricky said. "In fact, I don't like any of these. Every girl in the class will have practically the same thing." She turned to the saleswoman. "Don't you have something a little more—well, a little *different?*"

The woman raised her eyebrows. "But for ze graduation, my dear . . . ."

"What sort of dress were you thinking of?" Mrs. Parker asked gently.

Ricky did not answer, but walked toward another rack. She picked up a straight white lace gown, trimmed with rhinestone buttons. "Now that's more like it!"

The saleswoman turned to Mrs. Parker. "You sink a

dress like zat she should wear, your daughter?"

Ricky whirled around. "She's not my mother! And I know what I like! Where are the fitting rooms?"

The saleswoman shrugged. Ricky followed, then turned to Mrs. Parker and Donna. "Aren't you coming to see how the dress looks on me?"

"Maybe it won't fit," Donna whispered to her mother.

But according to Ricky, it was perfect. She ran her hands down the sides of the gown. "It looks as though I'd been practically *poured* into it," she said delightedly.

"Don't you think it's a little too bare looking for graduation?" Mrs. Parker asked, trying as hard but as tactfully as possible to discourage the girl.

"Everyone else is going to wear full skirts," Donna added, thinking of her own dress. "And won't that be hard to walk in? It looks sort of—" she searched for the right word, "—sort of *slinky*."

"Perhaps ze young lady could try on one of ze other gowns?" the saleswoman suggested. "Zis is after all for an older woman."

"I think it's perfect," Ricky repeated, turning to admire herself in the triple mirror. "And it will be just the thing to wear on the boat. I'll take it," she said decisively.

"Do you see what I mean?" Donna said, as she walked into her house that night. After the shopping, they had gone on to the ballet, followed by a quick supper at a restaurant near the station, for no one had been very hungry. Then they had taken the train back to Summerfield, where Mr. Parker had met them and taken Ricky home.

"About what?" Mrs. Parker asked, removing her hat.

"About Ricky." Surely now her mother could see how Ricky had changed. "I know you told me that clothes and things are important to her, Mommy. But she could at least show a little sense, couldn't she? You and I both know that she'll look foolish in that dress, and she wouldn't even listen to us. Why would she want to buy anything like that? She's becoming absolutely *impossible*, Mommy."

Mrs. Parker sat down on the sofa and took off her shoes. She wiggled her toes and sighed.

"I'm too exhausted to go over the whole thing with you, Donna. We've both had an exciting and a tiring day."

"But don't you agree, Mommy?" Donna insisted.

Mrs. Parker shook her head. "Donna, Ricky got up one morning and found her whole world had changed. Not a little change, but a big one, and a permanent one. Everything looks different to her now, so she wants to look different too. I'm sure she has no idea how she appears to other people. She probably doesn't even care. She's only worried about herself right now."

"But does she have to act so foolish, Mommy? One of these days she's going to wake up, and how will she feel then?"

"That depends on what she's like deep down, Donna. If she's a fine person, she'll face up to it and decide to change. As I hope you would do."

"Me?" Donna was shocked. "But I'd never get into a situation like that in the first place."

"We all do, sooner or later," Mrs. Parker said with a note of sadness in her voice. "And though I certainly don't want you hurt in any way, Donna, I almost wish something would happen that would make you a little less severe in your criticisms of people."

So maybe indirectly it was her mother who was the cause of the whole thing, Donna was to think later.

CHAPTER 13   *More Competition*

"It doesn't seem possible," Donna said, looking around at the rows of olive-green lockers. "I never thought I'd feel sentimental about this old locker room. But now that we're so close to leaving junior high forever, it almost begins to feel like home."

Anne Franklin groaned. "For the first day of school after vacation, you're certainly getting homesick early, Donna. We still have an awful lot of school left."

Karen's china-blue eyes widened. "All I can think of is exams. Do you know, in just a few weeks we'll be taking our *final* final exams? And those will be the marks that go on to senior high." She shuddered. "Although of course there are some people who can get all *A*'s and hardly have to study at all." She made a gesture toward Joyce Davenport, who was loading her arm with books from her locker.

"Me? Oh, I hardly think about marks any more," Joyce answered, turning around and facing the other girls. "But then, I'm not trying to get an award, or even a trip to California."

"It would be so much easier if you didn't have—certain competition," Karen whispered, first looking around to see that the "certain competition" was not in sight. They all knew that she meant Ricky.

"What I don't understand," Joyce said, shifting her books to her other arm, "is how you can be so nice to her, Donna."

Donna looked at Joyce. Was she being sarcastic?

"What do you mean?" she asked hesitantly.

"Oh, you know. Yesterday she called me up to tell me all about her trip to New York with you, and the bee-u-tiful gown she bought."

They would see the gown soon enough, Donna thought. She didn't have to say a word.

"And she told me about your taking her to lunch and the ballet," Anne added.

"How could you do it, Donna?" Karen asked. "Gee, you certainly have a kind heart. No matter how sorry I felt for someone, if she were my rival I couldn't be so sweet."

"Oh, it wasn't anything." She couldn't very well tell them that the whole trip had been her mother's idea, and that she had invited Ricky most reluctantly.

"I don't want to discuss it any more," she said in a tone of finality. "I didn't do anything."

The girls looked at her in admiration.

"Gee, there goes the bell," Joyce said, quickly shutting her locker and turning the combination.

"Come on, girls," came a boy's voice from the hall. "Leave it to the ladies to be late the first day of school."

"Ooh, that's Tommy Sheridan," Karen squealed. "He's in my first class. Maybe he'll carry my books for me."

"Karen!" Donna called. It was all right to have a boy carry your books, but how could she run after him that way? Karen, however, had disappeared.

"Hi, Donna," Bill Blanchard said as she hurried toward her algebra class. "Did you have a nice vacation?"

"Sort of, I guess," Donna replied without much enthusiasm.

Bill nodded. "I know what you mean. It certainly was a shame about Ricky's mother, wasn't it? And I guess it's been awfully hard on you, too, since you're her closest friend and all."

Goodness, wouldn't anyone let her alone? All they could do was talk about Ricky.

But algebra, and history, and English were difficult enough to make her concentrate completely on the class work, and forget her other troubles.

"Newspaper staff meeting after school," Tommy Sheridan reminded her as they passed in the hall between classes.

Donna nodded. They would have to begin planning the senior issue pretty soon, and that always meant a lot of extra work. She had better begin looking around, so she would have at least a few ideas in time for the meeting.

"Donna, do you want to be on the committee for Blue Jean Day?" George Hart, the president of the class, asked her as they stood in line to get their hot plates in the crowded lunch room. Yeeks, how could she be on that, and the newspaper, and still have time to study?

On the other hand, the more committees she was on, the more of a leader she would be. And leadership was one of the main requirements for the Outstanding Girl award.

"If you'd like to have me," she replied in answer to George's question. After all, Blue Jean Day was so much fun—the only day when they could wear dungarees and old clothes to school, and seniors took over most of the classes.

She carried her plate of frankfurters and baked beans to one of the long tables, where she was greeted with cries of welcome. It was wonderful to be back at school, and graduating. She had forgotten that life could be so exciting.

"Gee, it's good to see you, Donna," Sally Graham said. She moved over, to make room for Donna on the long bench. "Say, a messenger was in here looking for you a few minutes ago. He left this note for you. I told him I'd be responsible for your getting it."

Donna unfolded the yellow slip of paper. "It's from Mrs. Thomas. She says she wants to see me after school today."

"The dean of girls?" Sally looked surprised. "Do you have any idea what it's about, Donna?"

Donna shook her head. What had she done now? Why was she wanted in the dean's office?

Her thoughts kept returning to the appointment all afternoon, and it was with trembling hands that she knocked on the door after school.

"You—you wanted to see me?" she asked timidly.

"Come in, come in, Donna," the gray-haired woman sitting at the desk said. "And don't look so scared, my dear." She motioned Donna to a chair. Then she smiled.

"I only wanted to tell you that you're one of the leading contenders for the Outstanding Girl award, and that we'll be watching you very carefully. Now that's nothing to be frightened of, is it?"

Donna relaxed. Was that all Mrs. Thomas had wanted? Well, since she was here, maybe some of her questions could be answered. "Could you explain something to me?" she asked hesitantly.

"Of course, my dear. What is troubling you?"

"I'm not sure about the way you decide who is eligible for the award, Mrs. Thomas. Do the teachers make the choices, or what?"

Mrs. Thomas nodded. "I'll explain that. You see, everything that you do in your senior year is worth a certain number of points. The grades on your report card are, of course, worth the greatest number; A's are ten points each, B's are five points each, and C's are only two points."

Donna listened intently, trying to remember every word Mrs. Thomas was saying.

"Then your activities are all given points, too. For instance, your being on the newspaper staff is worth five points. If you were editor, that would be another five points. Each committee that you are on gives you more points."

She paused. "Now do you understand, my dear?"

"I think so," Donna answered. "But what about attitude? Do you mark that too?"

Mrs. Thomas leaned back in her chair. "That's one thing on which we have to use our judgment, but you may be sure that we consider it very carefully." She stood up, as though to signify that the conversation was ending. "But that's one thing about which you need have no fear, Donna. Your attitude is always splendid."

Goodness, thought Donna, *that's not the way my mother feels!*

She came over to Donna and put a motherly arm around her shoulder. "We've heard how helpful you've been to Ricky in her hour of need, my dear."

Yeeks, Donna thought. *What an expression—her hour of need—and Ricky didn't seem to need anything or anyone.*

"Incidentally, you may be interested in knowing that Ricky and you seem about equal in your number of points so far. But I don't mind telling you this—because you've always been such good friends I'm sure the matter of a prize will never come between you."

Donna tried to smile. If Mrs. Thomas only knew!

"As for your marks, I certainly don't have to warn you to work as hard as you can. Keep an eye on that old demon algebra, and you'll be just fine."

Mrs. Thomas gently led Donna toward the door.

"Is—is that all?" Donna asked in a shaky voice.

"Yes, that's all, my dear. And once again, let me thank you for your kindness toward Ricky. Remember, if any of us can be of any assistance, don't hesitate to let us know."

"G-Good afternoon," Donna said simply, as she opened the door that led to the hall. She could never explain to Mrs. Thomas how she felt about Ricky. Her mother didn't understand, so how could a teacher? Thank goodness for Joyce and Anne and Karen!

To her surprise, Ricky was sitting on the bench outside the dean's office.

"Oh!" Donna said, as Ricky stood up. "Are you waiting to see Mrs. Thomas too?" Of course that was it. Now it was Ricky's turn to hear the dean's little speech. She wondered whether Mrs. Thomas would say anything about Ricky's attitude. Well, Joyce and the other girls could tell her a few things!

To her surprise, however, Ricky made no move toward the office.

"I was waiting for you, Donna," the red-haired girl said. "Sally Graham told me you were here. And we usually walk home together, you know."

Donna looked at her in amazement. Did Ricky really believe that things were just the same as they used to be?

"My father increased my allowance," Ricky said, apparently not noticing Donna's surprise. "And I thought I'd treat you to a sundae at the Sweet Shop."

So Ricky was trying to make friends! Maybe she was beginning to be sorry for the way she had been acting. Maybe she was beginning to come to her senses.

"I have to stop at the library on my way home, but I'd love to have a sundae with you first," Donna said.

Ricky looked pleased. Then she frowned. "Gee, Donna, I forgot my science book. It's in my locker. Will you wait here for me?" She started down the hall, then turned and came back. "I've got a better idea. Suppose you go ahead to the Sweet Shop and get a booth for us. If I'm not there by then, order a butterscotch sundae with lots of whipped cream for me."

Donna nodded agreement. The Sweet Shop was always so crowded after school that it would surely take a little while to be waited on. At least this way she would still have time to go to the library.

Donna walked down the long corridor toward the main doors. Gee, maybe Ricky was returning to her usual sweet, thoughtful self. Maybe they could really be friends again, the way they used to be.

Going from the dark hall into the bright light of the outdoors made her squint. As she went down the broad stone steps, she hardly noticed a boy walking along the path toward her.

He seemed to be smiling at her. "Hmph!" she thought, raising her chin higher. She knew those senior high boys who thought that, because they were a little older, the junior high girls should feel flattered at any attentions.

Suddenly she stopped. It was Paul! Whatever was he doing here at the junior high? Would he even say hello to her, after the way she had spoken to him on the telephone?

Her heart gave a little skip. She had never really noticed how handsome he was. He had such broad shoulders, and carried himself so well. His skin was tanned and outdoorsy looking, and the hair on his forehead, where it came down into a deep widow's peak, was so blond that it was almost platinum. It was hard to believe she had really gone out with him twice. Whatever had made her speak to him the way she had?

She stepped aside to let him pass, but he stopped directly in front of her. "Gee, Donna, this is luck. I tried to get here before school closed, so I wouldn't miss you, but I couldn't."

Donna was speechless. Had Paul really come to the junior high just to see her?

"Then you're not—not angry at me?" she asked.

"Angry?" Paul looked at her in astonishment. "Oh, you mean about your not going to the movies with me when I asked you."

Donna started slowly down the path toward the street. "I'd like to—well, explain, about that, Paul," she said in a low voice.

"Oh, you don't have to," the boy replied. "Here, I'll carry your books." She had forgotten how well mannered he was. "Of course I was a little disappointed at the time. But then I thought over what you had said, and I decided you were absolutely right."

Donna gasped. "I was?"

They stopped again at the end of the path, and faced each other.

"Absolutely," Paul repeated. "You told me that if it

was so important for me to earn money that I wanted to leave school to do it, then I certainly shouldn't spend it on luxuries like movies. And Donna," he continued, his blue eyes looking directly into her brown ones, "I want to tell you that there aren't many girls who would be so thoughtful."

"Thoughtful?"

"Most girls are so anxious to have fellows spend money to take them out, that nothing else is important to them. But thank goodness you're different. I could tell that you're interested in *me,* not just in having dates. So I wanted to ask you, Donna . . . ."

"Ask me what, Paul?" she said softly.

"Ask you if I couldn't see you sometimes anyhow. Oh, I wouldn't spend any money," he added hurriedly. "I just mean things like going for a walk, or maybe coming over to your house once in a while."

Donna nodded. "Of course we can see each other, Paul. I'd like that," she said. "If you have a few minutes now, maybe you could walk to the Sweet Shop with me."

"Sure thing." The boy swung over to the street side, as they turned in the direction of the shop. "Gee, Donna, I have so much to tell you."

"About school?" she asked hesitantly. "Have you made up your mind yet, Paul?"

"I decided to give my father until the end of spring vacation to find a job. And this morning, when he still didn't have anything at all, I went to school and told them I was leaving."

"You've definitely decided?" Donna asked in a disappointed tone. What a shame!

"Gee, Donna, I feel worse about it than anybody else. It was just awful to leave Summerfield Senior High, and realize that I'll probably never go back to it. And I had no idea how complicated it would be to quit."

"What do you mean?"

"Well, I had to get permanent working papers, and have them signed by the school and by Mr. Davenport. By the way, he's been wonderful about it. Even though I was supposed to start work on the newspaper today, he let me have the day off to get everything finished. And he told me about a high school course that I can get through the mail and receive full credit for. So eventually I will get a high school diploma, anyhow."

Paul was silent for a moment. "I already had a social security card; otherwise that would have taken another couple of hours. And, Donna, there's one other thing I wanted to mention to you." He slowed his steps.

"What's that?"

"About my name. Oh, you know," he went on, in obvious embarrassment. "I mean about calling me Paul. That's another thing you did for me, Donna."

"I did? Why, what do you mean?"

"After I told you about it, I realized that there was no reason now to keep using Richard as my name. So I told them at the newspaper office to call me Paul, too. Of course," he looked at her warningly, "I'm sure you won't tell anyone about why I changed from Paul to Richard."

"But suppose they ask?"

"Just tell them I've been using my middle name, and now I've gone back to my first name. Which is the truth."

Suddenly, as they crossed the street in front of the Sweet Shop, Paul turned and smiled at her.

"Gee, I'm glad I met you," he said. "I feel better when I talk to you. But that's enough of my troubles. Say, some of the fellows told me that they saw you at the bowling alley during vacation. I didn't know you could bowl, Donna."

Donna made a face. "It's not what anyone would call

bowling," she laughed. "But it's fun, and maybe some day I'll learn, so I won't be ashamed to be seen in public."

"I wish I could teach you," he sighed. "But I guess those things are ended for me—at least for a while."

Donna looked at the boy by her side admiringly. Imagine how differently people acted when there was trouble. On the one hand there was Ricky, who now thought only of herself, of her clothes, of her trip, of her prizes. Even the sundae she was going to buy came from an allowance she must have demanded from her eager-to-please father.

And on the other hand there was Paul. He was so noble, so sacrificing, giving up school which meant so much to him, giving up almost all his pleasures and entertainment. You never knew how people would react, she thought, gazing up at him.

"Well, here we are," Paul announced, handing Donna's books back to her. "Thanks for letting me walk with you."

"Oh, thank *you*," Donna answered.

"Do you think I could see you this weekend?" Paul asked. "I might have to work on Saturday, but I'm sure I'll have Sunday free. Or—or would that be too soon?"

"Too soon?" Why, it was almost a week until Sunday! "Oh, no, that would be fine."

Then she added, "Paul, I have an idea. Daddy said that the color films that he took in India would probably be ready by Saturday night, and he'd show them to us on Sunday afternoon. Why don't you come and see the movies? I'm sure Mother and Daddy won't mind at all."

"Gee, Donna, that would be wonderful."

"Why, Donna," said Ricky's voice behind her, suddenly. "You haven't even gotten us a booth yet."

Donna turned, flushing. "I—I happened to meet Paul White," she said. "You two know each other, don't you?"

"Of course," Paul said. "We met at Camp Cherrydale last summer. In fact, I was just asking Donna about you the other night, Ricky. Well, I'd better be going now. See you on Sunday, Donna. Should I call to see whether your parents say it's all right?"

"Oh no," Donna answered. "I'm sure it will be fine."

The two girls entered the Sweet Shop.

"Gee, I didn't know you were seeing him, Donna," Ricky said as they slipped into a booth. "Did you call him Paul? I thought his name was Richard."

"Oh, it's both," Donna said airily. "His first name is Paul, and his middle name is Richard, and he just told me that now he's decided to go back to his first name." There, she had gotten through that all right. Ricky seemed satisfied with the explanation.

"Gee, he's cute," Ricky said dreamily. "Did I hear you say something about Sunday?"

Donna nodded. "Paul said he'd come over on Sunday afternoon. Daddy's going to show us the color films that he took in India."

Ricky leaned forward. "Oh, they must be thrilling, Donna. I'd love to see them too."

What could she say? Donna thought.

"Well, of course, if you'd like to come over . . ." she replied, not very enthusiastically. Ricky seemed not to notice her tone.

"Gee, I'd love to, Donna."

Although Ricky wanted to stay at the Sweet Shop and chat after they had their sundaes, Donna apologized and said she had to leave in order to do her work at the library.

"Of all things!" she thought, idly pulling a book from the library shelf. "Practically inviting herself to my house for Sunday afternoon."

She put the book under her arm, and ambled over to the large round table where she was working. "I wonder whether she's interested in the films—or in Paul!"

CHAPTER 14   *Joyce Tries to Help*

"And to think I stayed up half the night doing algebra," Donna said to Joyce, as they joined the boys and girls headed for the school auditorium. "I completely forgot that we have a long assembly this morning, and we'll miss first period."

"Half the night?" Joyce laughed. "Gee, Donna, you must have had your mind on something else, because we had very little homework for algebra."

In a way, Joyce was right. How could she possibly concentrate, with her mind on a million other things? And math had always been her most difficult subject.

"That may be true, but Daddy couldn't do it, either," she informed Joyce. "He remembers an awful lot about it, and he can usually explain it to me, but this time even he was stumped. And gee, Joyce, I've just got to get all *A*'s."

Joyce seemed about to say something. She closed her lips tightly, then turned and blurted out, "Donna, I hope you don't misunderstand me. I'm not any smarter than you are, but algebra is easy for me. Would you mind—I mean, would you let me help you?"

"Mind?" Donna squeezed the girl's arm. "Golly, Joyce, it would be just wonderful if you would. And don't worry so much about people thinking you're too smart. Could you come over after school and help me?"

"I'd love to. Today's the newspaper meeting, you know, but I could come tomorrow."

"Ssh!" Donna whispered, as they entered the auditorium. "They're getting ready to salute the flag."

The two girls slid into their places as the introduction to "The Star-Spangled Banner" filled the now-quiet auditorium.

At the final words of the pledge of allegiance, and the subsequent small noises as the students seated themselves, Donna tapped the shoulder of Anne Franklin, who was directly in front of her.

"Why the long assembly?" she asked under her breath. "Movies?"

Anne turned her head slightly, and out of the corner of

her mouth answered, "No, silly. Teacher's Assembly."

Donna leaned back. How could she have forgotten? This was the program, held once a year, that the boys and girls enjoyed most of all, when the teachers got up on the stage and performed. It was amazing how human they looked, too—not at all like teachers.

She knew that Miss McLaughlin always recited *The Highwayman,* and Mr. Oldenburg played the piano. But sometimes the other teachers would do a play, or a minstrel show.

This year several of the faculty, under the supervision of Mr. Detweiler of the English Department, put on *Pyramus and Thisbe,* from *A Midsummer Night's Dream.* Donna thought she had never laughed so much in all her life.

"Not even when I saw that funny movie with Paul," she thought at the end of the assembly. "But at least here I didn't have to worry about acting ladylike. Everyone laughed as hard as I did."

"Gee, that was fun. What a wonderful way to start the morning!" Tommy Sheridan said to Donna as they left the auditorium. "It's a shame we can't do that every day."

And miss algebra in the bargain, Donna thought. It was awfully nice of Joyce to offer to help her, she mused. She would have to thank her again when she saw her at the meeting this afternoon.

On her way to the newspaper office after school, however, she was stopped in the hall by George Hart.

"You did say you'd be on the Blue Jean Day committee, didn't you, Donna?" he asked. She nodded. "It's right before exams, you know, so we don't have much time."

Donna sighed. The weeks certainly did fly.

"Anyhow," George continued, "there will be a meeting tomorrow after school in Mr. Greer's office. Try to be on time, will you, because it will probably be a long session."

She nodded again, and continued on her way toward the newspaper office. "Yeeks!" she thought suddenly. "Tomorrow is the day that Joyce is supposed to come and help me with the algebra. Oh, dear, what'll I do?"

She shrugged. Being on the committee probably meant several points toward the award. She would simply have to attend the meeting. "I'm sure Joyce will understand," she said to herself. "And I'll ask her to come on Thursday instead. After all, one more day of not understanding algebra won't make that much difference."

"Gee, Donna," Joyce said, "I don't know whether I can come on Thursday. I might have to go over to my father's office to help him with some extra work."

"Oh?" Donna asked with a rising inflection. "I didn't know you were still working for the *Bulletin*."

"This is something special," Joyce explained. "Daddy's secretary is ill, and she called yesterday to say she didn't know whether she'd be able to be back at work by Thursday. I promised my father that if she was still sick, I'd go in and help out."

"That's all right," Donna said. "Anyhow, it'll certainly be more fun for you doing that instead of going over my miserable algebra. Oh, I was only kidding," she added hurriedly, noticing the girl's hurt expression. "I just meant that *I'd* rather be working at your father's office."

Joyce smiled. "Incidentally, I've got some news for you about the *Bulletin*. Remember the boy who went to the camp near yours last summer? The one who led the band at our spring dance? Well, he's working for my father full time now!"

"I know," Donna said simply.

Joyce raised her eyebrows. "You do? How did you find out? He only started to work there today."

"Oh, we talked about it last week. Of course, he wasn't sure then, but he told me after school yesterday."

Suddenly Donna noticed that there was silence in the room. Everyone seemed to have stopped what he was doing, and was listening to her. She could feel the blush creeping over her face all the way up to her hairline.

"Well, I happened to see him after school," she said indignantly. "Is there anything wrong with that?"

"Of course there's nothing wrong," Joyce soothed her. "My father says he's a very nice boy, and a hard worker. And he did beautifully at school, too. It's a shame he had to leave."

Some of the other girls had gathered around them. "It's just that we didn't know you were so friendly with him, Donna," one of them said. The others nodded agreement.

"Tell us about him," Karen pleaded. "Is he really as nice as they say? I know he was president of his class, and got wonderful marks in all his subjects, and won awards."

"Why did he have to leave school?" Mary Jefferson asked.

Donna turned away. "What a lot of silly questions! Do you expect me to be able to answer all of them? Anyhow—" she picked up a pile of papers from Joyce's desk and moved away, "anyhow, I have a lot of work to do if I'm to get out of here before dark. Joyce, do you have those ballots that have to be given out, so that we can choose the most popular people in the class?"

She had successfully changed the subject, she realized, though she knew that eventually she would be asked again. For the present, however, everyone had turned to the work at hand.

The afternoon flew. "Thank goodness we got all that out of the way," Joyce said as she left the office with Donna, Anne Franklin, and Karen. "Tommy Sheridan said he'd take some pictures of the seniors to put in this last issue, and Mary is going to write the class history. Jack Kingston will write a special column about seniors in the various sports, and you have the ballots for Most Popular, and Best Looking, and Class Clown, and all that, don't you, Donna? I don't think we've forgotten anything, have we?"

"How about Ricky's assembly?" Karen asked. "Do you think we should have an article about it? That is, if she ever gives it. I forgot to mention it at the meeting."

"Ricky's assembly?" Donna asked, puzzled.

"Oh, I keep forgetting you're not in our English class, Donna," Joyce apologized. "Anyhow, it only happened this morning."

"I don't understand." What were they talking about?

This morning had been the Teachers' Assembly.

"Well, you know that Mr. Detweiler, our English teacher, is also in charge of the drama club that Ricky's in."

"Go on," Donna urged.

"I'm trying to," Karen said. "After class today, Ricky went up to Mr. Detweiler—we heard her, didn't we, Anne —and she said that since everyone had enjoyed the Teachers' Assembly so much, couldn't we have a Senior Assembly, a talent show with members of the senior class as performers. And she said she'd just lo-ove to direct it."

"She also said," Anne chimed in, "that she'd not only choose the talent, but she'd write sort of a show to tie it together—a trip around the world, or something, with the performers doing an act in each country."

"You mean like a hula dance in Hawaii?" Donna asked.

The girls giggled. "I don't think Mr. Greer would let them do a hula dance," Joyce said, "but that's the general idea. You know, a calypso singer from Trinidad, and a jig from Ireland."

"In fact," Anne added, "in just a few minutes she had Mr. Detweiler giving her permission to use the auditorium this afternoon, to try out some of the people for it."

"Gee, it'll be an awful lot of work," Donna said.

"Well, I know why she wants to do it," Karen said glumly. "She's just trying to get the award, and she figures that this will put her ahead of anyone else."

Donna stopped at the stair landing. "I guess she will get a lot of points for doing it," she said thoughtfully.

"Do I hear music?" Karen put up a finger for quiet. Sure enough, sounds were coming from the auditorium.

"Let's see what she's doing," Anne whispered. They walked softly toward the auditorium doors and quietly opened one.

The curtains on the stage had been pulled aside, and several people were standing there. A boy holding a guitar, one foot up on a wooden chair, was talking to someone in the front row.

"There's Armando," Karen whispered. "He's a wonderful guitar player and singer. And ooh, there's Ricky in the middle of the front row. What's she getting so excited about now?"

"But I can't play with my foot up like that, Ricky," Armando was complaining. "Why can't I just sit down, the way I always do?"

"Because you're supposed to be a wandering minstrel," Ricky said, and in the empty auditorium her voice carried back to the girls on waves of echoes. "Why can't you understand that sometimes what *feels* natural doesn't *look* natural? Now try it again, Armando," she finished wearily.

The girls closed the auditorium doors, and walked silently down the corridor.

"That Ricky wants to be the whole show," Karen said at last. "Pretty soon people are going to get tired of having her boss them around, even if they do want to be nice to her because they're sorry for her."

"Oh, what does she care," Anne said. "As long as she gets her points and wins the award, so she can go to Europe."

"Well, she does have some good ideas," Donna admitted. "And she has a terrific imagination." It seemed so long ago that the two of them had had those wonderful conversations. Ricky had always managed to make life exciting and romantic.

"Now, Donna," Karen warned, "remember what you told us. You've simply got to win that prize."

"I've been thinking," Joyce said. She had remained quiet during the conversation. "Donna, there's one thing that you can do that I'm certain will give you a lot of extra points, too."

The girls all turned toward Joyce. "You usually get an *A* in English, don't you, Donna?"

Donna nodded. Why did Joyce want to know?

"I guess the teachers will announce it pretty soon, but this will give you a head start."

Whatever was Joyce talking about?

"Don't you remember from the other graduating classes, Donna? Everyone who gets an *A* in English is eligible to try out for valedictorian."

"Vale—*who?*" Karen asked.

"It means the person who gives the farewell speech at graduation," Joyce explained. "You know, a lot of schools just pick the person with the highest marks to make the speech. But here at Summerfield, every senior who wants to, and who has an *A* in English, is allowed to write a speech."

"And who chooses the best one?" Karen asked.

"The teachers who have the ninth grade English classes, I think," Joyce explained. "And maybe Mr. Greer, too—I'm not sure. But I am sure that it's quite an honor to be chosen, so it must mean a lot of extra points. Donna, you've just got to be the valedictorian."

"I? Write a speech?" Donna asked. "But with all my other work, how will I ever have time to do it? Anyhow, we're not even sure of the rules—how long it should be, or what it should be about, or anything."

"Gee." Joyce looked worried. "Maybe I can find out, Donna. And when I come over to your house we can talk about it again."

By Thursday two things had happened. First, as Joyce had predicted, Miss Griffith had announced the contest for valedictorian, and given all the *A* students a mimeographed copy of the rules, including not only the topics and the length, but also the closing date.

Secondly, Joyce told Donna that Mr. Davenport's secretary was well, and back at the office, and she would be able to come over as they had originally planned.

"Now," Donna said, as the two girls settled themselves cross-legged on her bed. "Do we do the algebra first, or do we try to write the speech first?"

"Let's begin with something I'm sure of," Joyce decided, opening the schoolbook that lay between them. "What part bothers you most, Donna?"

Donna threw her hands up toward the ceiling. "Start any place," she said. "Just pick a page."

Quickly Joyce ruffled through the book. "Well, you must understand what we had at the beginning of the year.

Let's see, how about this problem that we had yesterday?"

Donna picked up a pencil, and chewed on the end. She wrote some figures on a sheet of paper, then looked at Joyce for approval.

Joyce shook her head. "See, here's where you got all confused. Let's change this, and—"

At that moment there was a knock on the bedroom door. "I'm sorry to disturb you, dear," Mrs. Parker said, "but this just came for you." She held out a large box.

"For me?" Donna gasped.

"And this came, too, by special messenger." Mrs. Parker handed her daughter an envelope, the front of which was almost covered by stamps.

"It's a special delivery letter, Mommy! Oh, which one should I open first?"

CHAPTER 15 *The Dream Comes True*

Donna examined the large flat cardboard box. Then she looked at the letter. Both contained Bunny Knight's name, and return address.

"Here, I'll take the letter," Joyce suggested. "Then you can open the box."

Donna pulled at the string, removed the lid and several layers of tissue, and then both girls gasped.

"My bridesmaid dress!" Donna squealed. "I knew it! I knew it!"

"Could you—take it out of the box?" Joyce asked wistfully.

"Try it on, dear," Mrs. Parker suggested. "The reason Bunny sent it was so that you could see how it fits."

"Right now? Oh, I'd *love* to!" Swiftly Donna stripped off her blouse and skirt, then tenderly took out the pale organdy gown and held it at arm's length.

"Oh, it's just darling," Joyce said.

Donna quickly put it on, and smoothed the full skirt that fell in rich folds over yards of taffeta. Then she ran to her mirror. "Ooh, it fits perfectly, doesn't it, Mommy? I've got to see what it looks like in your long mirror."

The two girls ran to Mrs. Parker's bedroom, and Donna pirouetted before the glass.

"It *is* perfect, isn't it, Mommy? But don't these clumsy old shoes look silly with it? Oh, what'll I do about slippers? I never thought of that."

"How about opening the letter?" Mrs. Parker asked. "Perhaps Bunny has further instructions in it."

Both girls ran back to Donna's bedroom.

Donna quickly read the note, then nodded to her mother. "You're right. She asks if I won't please get plain pumps that can be dyed the same color as the gown. May I, Mommy?"

"I guess you'll have to. Maybe we can go down to the shoe store on Saturday. And the dress does look lovely on you, dear," Mrs. Parker added approvingly.

Donna carefully took off the gown, and hung it in her

closet. Mrs. Parker left, and Joyce opened her algebra book.

But Donna could not seem to put her mind to the work. "Gee," she complained, "now my head's full of the wedding, and all the other things I have to do—the valedictory, and Blue Jean Day, and the newspaper." She slammed the book shut. "Oh, Joyce, how will I ever get this through my head?"

"Was your uncle really serious about your marks, Donna? Maybe he was just teasing about your not going to California if you didn't do well at school."

Donna looked at Joyce, her eyes wide. "He wasn't teasing at all. He was very serious. He thinks Daddy would blame my marks on him." She gazed into space, as though trying to see what the future would hold. "Oh, it would break my heart if I didn't go to California this summer."

Then she tapped her pencil against the book. "What would I do if I didn't go? It would spoil my whole summer." Suddenly she jumped up. "Oh my goodness, I forgot all about Dr. Duval. I have to tell him whether I'm going back to Cherrydale. I'd better call right away and make an appointment to talk with him."

She paused at the door to her room. "Gee, Joyce, I'm

sorry there are so many interruptions. But I'll only be a minute, and then maybe we can work."

In a few moments she was back. "Dr. Duval said I could see him on Saturday. I'm glad I'll get that out of the way, though I haven't the faintest idea what I'll say to him. Now, where were we?"

This time Donna almost succeeded in pushing all other thoughts from her mind.

"Thanks ever so much, Joyce," she said as the girl left. "You've really helped me a lot."

"Oh, it was nothing," Joyce answered. "Good luck to you on Saturday, with Dr. Duval."

Donna stood at the front door for a little while. How would she ever explain her complicated situation to the doctor?

But the interview on Saturday was surprisingly easy.

"Well, now," the doctor said when he had heard her story. "My wife and I had thought of your coming back as a junior counselor. That would mean being at camp from the beginning of July until almost the end of August, and would leave you no time for California."

"If I go," Donna added.

"You may recall," the doctor continued, "how difficult

it was last year to make arrangements when several of
the counselors had their days off in August, and other
people had to substitute for them."

Donna nodded, but remained silent.

"So we've been considering the idea of having an extra
person just for August, to take over for the girls who
are off duty." He leaned back in his chair. "If you were to
be that person, you would only come to camp for one
month, and you would have July free. Would one month
be enough for your trip?"

"Yes, indeed. Oh, Dr. Duval, that would be just perfect."
Her mind was working quickly. Then even if she didn't
go to visit her uncle, at least she wouldn't be spending the
whole summer at home. "And I'm sure I could do the
work."

"Of course you could. Well, that's settled then. Please
call me when school is finished, and I'll tell you exactly
when to report to Cherrydale."

Donna rose and shook hands with the doctor. "Wait'll I
tell Mommy and Daddy," she thought as she walked home.
"What a wonderful solution to my summer problems. Of
course," she admitted to herself a little sadly, "Cherrydale
won't be the same, since Paul won't be at Camp Three

Pines, and we won't have any camp dates like we had last year."

Her thoughts strayed to Paul. "Why, tomorrow's Sunday," she realized with a shock. "He'll be coming over to see the movies. And Ricky too," she added sourly. "Well, maybe Paul will come much earlier than Ricky."

That was not, however, the way things happened. Paul had no sooner rung the doorbell on Sunday afternoon, than Ricky was walking up the front steps.

"Goodness, that doesn't even give me a chance to have one word alone with him," Donna thought.

"Come in, come in," Mr. Parker called from the living room, where he was threading film into a projector. "Paul, I hope you know something about these machines. Is this loop big enough? I'd hate to break the film."

"Why can't I help, Pop?" asked Jimmy, bending his head down to join the other male heads.

Mr. Parker looked up. "We're doing just fine, James my boy. Tell you what—why don't you begin pulling down the shades so that it's dark in here? We'll never be able to see the movies with all this sunshine streaming in."

"Gee, Pop," Jimmy reported a few minutes later. "Even with the shades down it's still too light."

"Daddy, should I get some old blankets to hang over the window?" Donna suggested. At her father's preoccupied nod, she went off to look for blankets.

She half expected to find Ricky deep in conversation with Paul when she returned. But to her surprise, Ricky seemed not to have moved.

"Hm," she thought. "If she was so anxious to see him, why isn't she talking to him?"

She proceeded to hang the blankets so that the windows were covered.

"Now, that's better," Ricky said. "It's almost as dark as night in here."

"Are you almost ready, dear?" Mrs. Parker asked anxiously. "It's getting a little stuffy, with all the doors and windows closed."

"Ready!" Paul announced. "I think that'll be all right now, Mr. Parker."

There was silence, and all eyes turned toward the sheet that had been hung from the mantelpiece. A picture appeared, a little too high and slightly blurred, but Mr. Parker quickly adjusted the projector.

"There!" he said with a sigh of relief. "Now it's fine." Everyone murmured agreement.

"Ooh, there's Mommy," Jimmy yelped.

"That's in Shannon, Ireland," Mr. Parker explained. "We stopped there and had a little breakfast. See the printing on that truck at the airfield? It's in Gaelic, the language they use in Ireland."

"This is Orly Field in Paris," Mrs. Parker commented. "That's where the plane had motor trouble. And here we are in Rome."

"Rome!" Ricky sighed. "That's one of the places my father and I are going this summer. Which hotel did you stay at, Mrs. Parker?"

"Here's the picture of our hotel," the woman answered. "It was a lovely place. We were so sorry it rained all the time we were in Italy, but we still managed to see a great deal."

"Oh, we're going to stay at a different hotel," Ricky said. "It's the largest one in Rome, and the most expensive."

Gracious! Donna thought. *Does she have to brag like that? Anyhow, how can she be so sure that she's going? Here I don't even know whether my marks will be good enough for me to go to California, and she's positive that she'll go to Europe.*

The reel ended with the Parkers landing in Bombay,

and everyone applauded when the lights were turned on so that Mr. Parker could change to the next roll.

"Sam, you did a wonderful job," Mrs. Parker said proudly. "For a borrowed camera, and the first time you've ever used color film, they were awfully good pictures."

Mr. Parker looked up from the projector. "This is our journey through India," he announced. "We went from Bombay to New Delhi, then all the way down to Madras, and all over the southern part of India."

There were comments, explanations, and cries of delight through the entire reel.

"Oh, it was wonderful," Donna sighed as Mrs. Parker raised the shades. "The colors were so beautiful, and everything looked so romantic."

"Well," said Ricky, "I guess India is much more *unusual* than Europe, but I'm sure Europe is romantic, too."

Gee, thought Donna. *All she can talk about is Europe. And I thought she came here to see Paul.*

"Thank you so much for letting me look at the films," Ricky was saying to Mrs. Parker. "I have a much better idea now of what to expect."

"Oh, are you going home?" Donna asked.

Ricky nodded. "I have a lot of lessons to do, you know.

And then I have to finish writing the play for the Senior Assembly. I'll see you at school tomorrow, Donna."

And I, Donna thought, as Ricky left, *have to do my speech. But I'd much rather talk to Paul.* It was strange, but she was almost disappointed that Ricky had paid so little attention to him. Had she really come only to see the films?

She turned to the boy, who did not seem to know whether he was supposed to leave or not. "You don't have to go too, do you, Paul?" she asked.

"Well . . . ." He hesitated. "Don't you have homework too, Donna?"

"Just a speech to write, and I haven't the faintest idea what I'm going to say." She looked at the tall blond boy. "Oh, you were valedictorian last year, weren't you? Do you remember what you wrote?"

He nodded. "Would you want me to try to help you, Donna? I don't promise I'd be much assistance, but I could give you a few suggestions."

Donna's eyes lit up. "That would be marvelous." This way she would be doing her work, and still talking to him. Wasn't it nice to have friends like Joyce and Paul?

They walked back into the living room, where Mr.

Parker was just putting the projector into its case.

"For one thing," Paul said, "the teachers always like you to use poetry, either at the beginning or the end of the speech."

"Poetry? Like what?"

"Well, I began with that old Longfellow one. You know:

> Lives of great men all remind us
> We can make our lives sublime,
> And, departing, leave behind us
> Footprints on the sands of time.

"And then I told about how we hoped that we had left some footprints on the sands at junior high, and how the teachers had helped us."

"But what do I do for a poem?" Donna asked. "These are the only poetry books we have." She led Paul over to the bookcase in one corner of the room, and took out several volumes.

They both leafed through the books. But nothing seemed exactly right.

Suddenly Donna let out a little cry. "How about this?" She quoted: *" 'I hear America singing, its varied carols I hear. . . .'* And then it tells about carpenters, and different kinds of people that make up America."

Paul nodded. "And you could tell about how we've all learned to help in making the song of America."

"And we've learned to sing in harmony—you know, to get along with the other voices," Donna said, becoming more excited by the idea. Then she paused. "But we don't all have to sing the same song," she continued thoughtfully. "We don't even always have to have harmony. You know, in some of that modern music there are all sorts of weird discords, and it makes the music more exciting."

"But you have to get used to it," Paul interrupted.

"I know. But after a lot of the same old tunes, once in a while a discord makes you sit up and take notice. It sort of comes as a shock, I guess. And once in a while a person who says something different makes you stop and think."

"Donna, you've got it," Paul said admiringly. "That speech will be absolutely great."

Donna smiled happily. "You were the one who made me think of it, Paul."

"Isn't Paul nice?" Donna asked at supper that evening. "And he's so smart, too. He helped me a lot with my speech this afternoon. It's such a shame he had to leave school."

Both Mr. and Mrs. Parker looked up. "Leave school?"

"I'm not supposed to tell anyone," Donna said, "but I guess he didn't mean parents." She explained about Paul's job at the newspaper office, and his reasons for quitting school. "Imagine having a father who won't even get a job, and lets his wife support the family," she finished.

Mrs. Parker put her fork down slowly. "Why, Paul's mother must be Harriet White who has that charming little shop on Main Street." She turned to her husband. "You know, dear. I pointed it out to you just the other day. I met her at a bridge party a few weeks ago. She's a charming person. I had a long conversation with her."

So her mother knew about Mrs. White! No wonder Paul felt so badly. Half of Summerfield must know that his mother was working!

"I hear she's simply marvelous as a decorator, Sam. Some of her friends have been urging her for years to start a little business, but she kept saying that she'd have to wait till her children were grown."

Donna sighed. "And then when her husband was out of work, she had to start anyhow."

"Why, no, dear." Mrs. Parker frowned. "You must have gotten the story confused. The reason she started to work was because the old man who had that little shoe repair shop went to live with his daughter, and she was able to rent the store from him. She told me she's had her eye on that place for years."

"But she doesn't really want to work, does she, Mommy?"

Mrs. Parker laughed. "She certainly seemed excited enough about it, Cooky. She said she felt like a new woman, getting out of the house and away from dishes and beds for a change." She turned to her husband. "Sam, don't you know her husband? I think she said his name was Gordon."

"Gordon White? I didn't realize that's who he was. Why, he was in my office only a few days ago."

"Really, Daddy? What's he like?" Donna pictured a carelessly dressed, red-faced man.

"Mr. White? He's an awfully nice guy. Smart, too." Mr. Parker paused and looked at Donna. "Do you mean to tell me that that's why Paul quit school? Why, Gordon White could have a job any time he wants one. He told me he was almost ready to sign a contract with a firm right here in town. In fact, come to think of it"—he turned to his wife— "he said he had tried to get his wife to go away for a little vacation first, but she was so interested in her new job she wouldn't leave."

He shook his head. "Kids certainly do get funny ideas. Why, from the way you talked, Donna, I thought the family was practically starving."

So did I, Donna thought. *That's the way Paul made it sound.* She was completely perplexed by this latest news. *I thought his father was a dreadful creature, and it was up to Paul to take the responsibility for the family. But it isn't that way at all!*

She was still worrying about it the next day, though she tried desperately to keep her mind on the work going on in her classes. "I can't understand it," she kept thinking, only half listening to what the teachers were saying.

Suddenly, as she was trying to solve a problem in algebra class, she remembered her dream of some weeks before.

"Paul was in it," she recalled. "He said he'd show me the way home, and he seemed so sure of himself. But after we had walked for a while, I realized that he was lost, and didn't have any idea where he was going, and he was just getting me more confused. That dream knew more about Paul than I did!"

She chewed on her pencil, her mind miles away from the classroom. "He seems to be as mixed up as Ricky," she thought sadly. "Oh, why are people so complicated?"

CHAPTER 16   *The Final Week*

"Donna!" exclaimed Mrs. Parker, as she opened the door to her daughter's bedroom. "I couldn't believe I really saw the light burning in here. Are you still studying, at this hour?"

Donna looked up from her book for a moment. "I simply have to finish this chapter, Mommy."

"But your exams don't start until Monday, Donna, and you've been studying all week. You've got to get some sleep, too, or you'll never be able to think clearly."

"Just let me do this, Mommy," Donna begged. "I'll only worry about it if I don't."

Mrs. Parker sighed. "Very well. But be sure your lights are out in fifteen minutes."

"As if I could sleep anyhow," Donna thought as she closed her book a little later. "There are just too many things to worry about. Not only exams, and trying to get the award, either. Thank goodness I finished writing the valedictory, and that much is out of the way. I wonder when the winner will be announced."

Her thoughts rambled on, as she undressed and absent-mindedly put up her hair in pincurls. "Wasn't it lucky that Paul helped me with the speech? What a silly thing it was for him to leave school, especially since he really didn't have to. I could hardly believe what Mommy and Daddy told me about the Whites, but it's all true."

She twisted a lock of hair around her finger, and jabbed a clip through it. She hadn't seen Paul since the day of the India movies. "Maybe I can still convince him to go back to school. After all, he hasn't missed very much so far."

She sighed. "Today is Thursday. One week from now I'll be packing for the wedding. And one week ago I was studying algebra with Joyce. Think of it—this was the first time I've ever done homework with anyone but Ricky."

"Ready for bed, Donna?" Mrs. Parker called.

"Almost, Mommy," Donna answered, tying a band around her head to keep the clips in place. Her "headache band," Mr. Parker called it.

"Why did Ricky have to change?" Donna thought as she

climbed into bed. "We were good friends for so many years. And I'll have to admit that, after all, I do miss her— the old Ricky," she added hastily, "not the new one."

She started to pull the blanket over her shoulders, then sat up suddenly. "Goodness," she thought, and half smothered a giggle. "I didn't turn off the light."

With the room in darkness, she climbed into bed again. "Oh, for heaven's sake!" she thought wearily. "I forgot to decide what to wear tomorrow, for Blue Jean Day. It's got to include something brown and white—that's the rule. Oh, well, I'll decide in the morning. I hope I'm not absent-minded then, and go to school in a blouse and skirt the way I do every other day."

The words of the school cheer, which were running through her mind when she awoke, reminded her of the special event.

> White and brown
> Let's go to town.
> Brown and white
> Fight, team, fight!

"Brown and white," she mused, standing in front of her open closet. "At least I have my saddle shoes."

She rummaged through her bureau drawers, coming up with nothing more exciting than two extra pairs of shoelaces, one brown, the other white.

"Maybe I can use them for a hair ribbon. Wait—I know!" Quickly she pulled her dark hair back in a bunch at the nape of her neck. "A pony tail!" she thought happily. "I haven't worn my hair that way for years, and I can tie it with the shoelaces." She surveyed the results in the mirror. "Not bad," she commented approvingly. "It's a shame I spent all that time making pin curls last night. I must remember to change my hair style more often. I wonder what the other girls will be wearing."

Of course there were the usual scarves, and hair ribbons, and crepe paper bands. The boys had blossomed out in brown and white caps, and woven belts, and oversized paper bow ties.

"Oh, your hair looks darling that way," Karen said to Donna in the locker room. "Have you seen Ricky? She must have gone out and bought a new pair of dungarees, and they're *brown* with white stitching. Did you ever?"

"And she's got a brown-and-white checked shirt to go with it," Anne added. "I guess she wanted to get all dressed up for her assembly this morning."

"Her assembly?" Donna asked. "Oh, you mean the senior one. Well, she's been working on it awfully hard. She's been in the auditorium every day after school for hours."

"It had better be good," Karen muttered, as they walked toward the auditorium. "She's practically been after the kids who are in it with a whip."

"It must mean a great deal to her," commented Joyce, who had joined them in the hall. "Oh, look, Jack Kingston is going to play the piano, instead of Mr. Oldenburg."

"It's *Senior* Assembly," whispered Karen. "The seniors are supposed to do everything."

Sure enough, George Hart took the place usually reserved for Mr. Greer, the principal, and introduced each act.

"Gee, I didn't know there was so much talent in our class," Donna thought as she watched the various scenes. "Where did Ricky ever find them all? Her hard work really shows, too. I guess she's a good director after all, even though she does get awfully bossy."

Ricky herself did not appear until the end of the program, when George Hart introduced her. She took a brief bow, then started to return backstage. But Mr. Greer stood up at that point, and after apologizing for intruding in a student production, made a short speech of thanks to the cast, and special mention of Ricky's efforts.

"Well," Donna thought, as everyone trooped out of the auditorium. "I guess she earned those extra points toward the award. I suppose I shouldn't count on being valedictorian, but, oh, I want to be so very much, especially now!"

"Donna," said Miss Griffith, at the beginning of English, "I wonder whether you'd mind taking over the class for this period."

Donna looked at the teacher in surprise. It was true that on Blue Jean Day a great many teachers let seniors lead their classes. But what was she supposed to do?

Miss Griffith held out a book. "There's a story here that I think the class would enjoy. It's called 'The Lady or the Tiger?' and I'd like you to read it to us." The teacher rose, motioned Donna to sit in her chair, and went, herself, to the back of the room.

Donna glanced at the first page, then the last, to see where it ended, and then began to read. In a few moments she was as engrossed in the story as the rest of class. When she finished, there was a pause.

"You mean—that's the end?" someone asked.

"But was it the lady or the tiger who came out?" everyone wanted to know.

Miss Griffith smiled, and walked to the front of the classroom. "That's one question you'll each have to answer for yourself." Then she turned to Donna. "You read that just beautifully, my dear, and your voice carried quite well. I'm sure we'll have no trouble."

"Trouble?" Donna asked.

"Oh, I suppose that you haven't been notified officially yet." The teacher hesitated. "But I may as well tell you now. Yesterday afternoon the three English teachers who have senior classes had their final meeting, and voted to make you class valedictorian!"

Donna gasped. The class applauded. Miss Griffith beamed.

"You wrote an excellent speech, Donna," the teacher said. "I'm proud to have you in my class. You and I will have to practice together the week before graduation, after Memorial Day. I'm sure it won't take long to memorize it."

Donna floated back to her seat. Valedictorian! With her name on the program and everything. Wouldn't her parents be proud! And it would mean those extra points, too. Wait until Ricky heard!

" 'I hear America singing,' " she kept repeating to herself for the rest of the day, and all during the weekend, no matter what else she was doing. "I wish Paul would call," she thought, "so I could tell him."

But Paul did not call until Sunday, his one day off from the newspaper.

"I thought maybe we could go for a walk," he suggested. "It's such a nice day, Donna."

"I know," she agreed. "And I'd love to, Paul, but I can't. I promised my mother I'd go to bed early tonight, because exams begin tomorrow. And I still have an awful lot of studying to do." She lowered her voice. "You know how important these marks are to me."

"Exams?" Paul repeated. "Golly, I forgot all about them, Donna. I remember how hard I used to study for them, but it seems so long ago."

"Gee," Donna thought. "He sounds as though he left school about ninety years ago. And I'll bet he misses it. Why in the world doesn't he go back before it's too late?" She wished she had time for a talk with him. Maybe he would change his mind about school.

Suddenly she remembered. "Paul, my speech was chosen! I'm valedictorian! Isn't that marvelous?" She stopped. Was she beginning to sound like Ricky?

Paul did not seem to think that she was bragging. "It's

wonderful!" he said enthusiastically. "I knew you could do it." Then he paused. "Well, I hope you do well in your tests. I'll call you again soon."

Donna replaced the receiver on the hook. "I forgot to tell him that I'm going to the wedding next week." Then she shrugged. "Oh, well. I can't think about the wedding now. I've got to concentrate on nothing but my school-work. Oh, how can I ever get through this next week? Will Thursday ever come?"

Thursday did come, and all too soon. "All that work, and all that studying," Donna sighed to her mother, "and it was all over in four short days."

"How do you think you did, dear?" Mrs. Parker asked.

Donna sat down at the kitchen table. "Well, English and history and Latin were easy. In science I think I got con-fused in one question, but I still did pretty well. And as for algebra, I'll just keep my fingers crossed. Even with all the help Joyce gave me, I'm still not sure about some of the problems."

"When will you know your marks?" Mrs. Parker asked.

"Not until next week, Mommy, after Memorial Day. That's when we get our reports. Classes are over now, you know. We only have graduation practice next week."

"And you have to rehearse your speech," Mrs. Parker reminded her.

Mommy's really glad that I was chosen valedictorian Donna thought. *I knew she would be. It's so nice to do things that make your parents proud of you.*

She went over to the refrigerator and poured a glass of fruit juice for herself. "I'm sorry Mommy won't see me at Bunny's wedding," she thought, eying her slender waistline as she sipped the juice. "I'll bet she'd be proud of me then, too." Donna could not know that even the thought of the wedding would later make her blush with shame.

"I think I'd better go up and begin packing," she said. "I hope I don't forget anything."

"You're taking the nine o'clock train to New York tomorrow morning, aren't you, dear?" Mrs. Parker looked at her daughter with a slightly worried expression. "And you know how to get to Nottingham, don't you?"

"Goodness, Mommy. Bunny wrote it all down in her last letter. It's really very simple, and I'm sure I won't get lost."

"Of course not, Cooky. And we'll take you to the station here in Summerfield." Mrs. Parker's frown deepened. "I do wish we could stay to put you on the train."

"Why can't you, Mommy?" Now Donna was concerned.

"It's that Memorial Day outing, dear. You know, the one the town has at the park every year, with races and games and refreshments for all the children."

"But gracious, Mommy. You certainly don't have to be there at nine o'clock in the morning, do you?"

"It's not for us, honey. It's for Jimmy. He's playing in the juniors' baseball game, and a long time ago we promised we'd come to see him. It never occurred to me it would be held at the same time that you would be leaving."

"Oh, well," Donna said, "I guess I don't mind waiting on the platform alone for a few minutes. Nothing can happen in such a short time."

In that respect, however, Donna was wrong. For she had just waved farewell to her parents, after many good-bys and numerous instructions from Mr. and Mrs. Parker, and much nudging from Jimmy who was afraid they would be late for his game, when someone called her name.

She turned. Running across the parking lot next to the station, and coming toward the platform where she was standing, was a familiar figure.

"Why, it's Paul!" she thought in amazement. "Goodness, from the way he's puffing it looks as though he's run all the way here. What can be the matter?"

CHAPTER 17   *Stranger in Nottingham*

"Golly," Paul panted, as he reached her. "I never thought I'd make it, Donna." He wiped his forehead.

"What's the trouble, Paul?" she asked, with concern.

The boy paused a moment to catch his breath. "I went to your house first thing this morning, Donna. Mr. Davenport called earlier, to tell me that one of his reporters was sick and that he wanted me to go to the Memorial Day outing at the park. You know, to get the names of the people who win the pie-eating contest, and the potato-sack race, and that stuff."

He took a deep breath. "I thought maybe you'd want to go with me, so I stopped on the way to the park. I rang and rang, and finally your next-door neighbor told me that your parents had driven you to the station."

"But why did you come here, Paul? I'm on my way to

New York, you know, and of course I can't go to the picnic. And you'll be late. Why did you ever run all the way here?"

There was a rushing noise along the tracks. "Golly!" Paul said. "Here comes your train." Then he fumbled in his pocket, and drew out a small box wrapped in gift paper. "I planned to give you this later, but please take it now."

The train was pulling slowly along the platform. Paul thrust the little package into Donna's hand, and picked up her suitcase.

"You'd better get on before the train leaves without you," he said, striding over to the steps where a conductor was standing. Donna followed him, still holding the box.

"But what's in it?" she asked, perplexed.

"Better get aboard, little lady," said the conductor. He boosted her up the first high step, and put her suitcase in the train vestibule.

He blew a whistle—two short tweets—and then hopped on the train himself. Donna stood at the top of the stairs, looking down at Paul.

"I hope you like it," the boy called as the train began to move. Donna nodded, and waved. Then she picked up her bag and went to find a seat.

Settled by a window, she picked up the package and

quickly unwrapped it. Inside lay a plain silver ring. "A ring!" Donna breathed. "A real friendship ring." She tried it on, and found that it fit perfectly. "Wasn't that sweet of Paul? And after all he said about not spending money, too."

She gazed at her finger thoughtfully. "I wonder what Mommy and Daddy will say." She frowned. Was it all right to accept a ring from a boy? Then the frown disappeared. She could at least wear it this weekend, until she got home. And it did make her feel so much more grownup. Somehow it seemed to give her poise and confidence.

The feeling continued all during the trip, as she changed trains in New York, arrived in Nottingham, and following Bunny's instructions, took a cab to the Knight home.

The taxi stopped in front of a charming Norman style house, with gabled roofs and leaded diamond-shaped windows, and a large expanse of lawn in front.

She paid the driver, walked up the winding flagstone path, and paused a moment before she rang the bell. Suddenly she felt completely alone. What was she doing here, all by herself? What kind of people were the Knights?

Even looking at Paul's ring, which she had begun to feel was like a good-luck charm, did not give her courage.

She put down her suitcase, sighed deeply, and timidly

rang the doorbell. She could hear footsteps inside.

In a moment the door was opened, and a tall slender woman, her gray hair elegantly waved, opened the door.

"You must be Donna Parker," she said warmly. "Come right in, my dear. I'm Bunny's mother. She'll be down in just a moment."

Donna looked around. The large living room was furnished simply with pine and maple and cherry pieces, and charming flowered chintzes covered the sofa and chairs. She turned at the sound of footsteps on the broad stairs, and in a flash Bunny had thrown her arms around her.

"Oh, darling! I'm so glad you're here. How wonderful of you to come all this way." She held Donna off at arm's length, and looked at her. "You haven't changed a bit since last summer," she said. "Mother, didn't I tell you she was just the sweetest thing?"

Mrs. Knight smiled. "I've got to finish arranging the gifts that arrived this morning, Bunny. I suppose we'll have to set up another table to display them on. You make Donna comfortable, dear."

"Would you like to see my gifts, Donna?" Bunny asked, obviously bursting with pride. Then she shook her head. "How thoughtless of me! Of course you want to go to your room first, and wash up after your trip. I'm so sorry we couldn't meet you at the station, but the cars are all on various errands."

Donna followed her hostess up the stairs.

"Here's your room, and this is Eloise Townsend, my cousin. Everyone calls her Ellie."

Donna smiled a greeting at a girl about her own age whose shoulder-length golden hair and pale skin contrasted with the short black leotard she was wearing.

"Oh, Ellie," Bunny said reproachfully. "You're not still doing those exercises! Why, you're not even dressed yet, and your mother is waiting to take you to Aunt Agatha's."

The girl continued to do deep knee bends, using the footboard of one of the twin beds as an exercise bar.

"I'll be through in a few minutes, Bunny. Mother knows that Professor will have my head if I don't keep limber." She waved her free hand at Donna. "Hi, and welcome. Do you mind taking the bed by the window?" She turned, and arched her back until she could touch her head with the sole of her foot.

Bunny showed Donna where to hang her clothes. "Come down as soon as you've unpacked, sweetie. Lunch will be very informal. Lucy is making piles of sandwiches, so just walk into the kitchen and help yourself." She ran her hand through her hair. "Even with Miss Boyle supervising the wedding, Mother and I are so busy we don't know what to do first. I hope you'll forgive us for not treating you more like a real guest. And don't mind Ellie. She goes to ballet school in New York, but otherwise she's perfectly normal."

Donna walked over to the window after Bunny left. "Oh, what beautiful grounds!" she said. "It looks almost like a park. Is that where the wedding is going to be?"

Ellie went over to the other window, put her foot on the sill and bent her head down to touch her extended leg. "The reception is going to be held there. Some men are coming this afternoon to put up a tent. But Bunny wanted to be married in the formal garden."

Donna looked. Which part was the formal garden?

"Oh, you can't see it from here," Ellie said, changing to her other leg. "And it really isn't a formal garden. It has evergreens all around it, to form a square, and a path down the middle, but Aunt Mary never got around to putting in rose bushes and things. You'll see it at rehearsal."

Donna supposed that Aunt Mary was Bunny's mother. She turned and opened her suitcase. Ellie had apparently decided either that she was limber enough, or that her mother would wait no longer, for she was changing into a cotton dress.

"That's the one trouble with visiting Aunt Mary. Every summer when Mother and I come here we have to make calls on my other relatives. Today it's Aunt Agatha."

"Oh, don't you live in New York?" Donna asked.

"No, I only go to boarding school there. It's a school for people who want to become professional dancers. But we live in Olympia, Washington, and Mother flies to New York every year when school is over to take me home, and that gives her a chance to visit the family."

She was acting, thought Donna, as though Washington were a million miles away, in another country!

"Oh, do you fly very much?" Donna asked, aloud. "My parents have just come back from India—that's halfway around the world, you know." Humph! That would show this Ellie person that other people used airplanes, too. What made her think she was so special, just because she went to a fancy ballet-boarding school?

"Really?" Ellie fastened her belt. "That must have been a wonderful trip. Do you like flying, too?"

Donna gulped. Ellie seemed to have a knack for making her feel so—so small. "I'm going to fly to California this summer, after I graduate." She didn't have to tell Ellie that the trip wasn't quite definite yet, did she?

"That'll be nice," Ellie answered. "What school are you graduating from?"

Donna hesitated. "Summerfield Junior High." She took out the organdy bridesmaid's dress, and put it on a hanger.

"Why don't you take that down to the kitchen when you go down?" Ellie suggested. "Lucy will press it for you." She ran a comb through her silky hair. "Sorry I have to leave, but I'll be back for the rehearsal. 'By now."

Donna was left alone in the room. She had expected to have a long talk with her roommate, to ask her about the other bridesmaids, and what she was supposed to do at the wedding, and a whole list of other things.

She unpacked, then washed and went downstairs.

"Do help yourself to the food in the kitchen," Mrs. Knight said, as she passed Donna in the hall.

"Is there anything I can do for you?" Donna asked Bunny, after she had finished a solitary lunch. Although there had been plenty of food, it hadn't seemed right to spend too much time eating, with everyone rushing around.

"Not a thing, darling. I have to get my hair done now, but the hairdresser promised that I'd be through and back here by three o'clock. Perhaps you'd like to rest, or read, or something. Just make yourself comfortable. And ask Lucy, if you need anything."

Donna smiled at Bunny, who seemed as jumpy as the brides she had read about. "I guess I'd be, too, if I were getting married tomorrow," she thought.

She ducked, as two men walked by her with large ladders. "I suppose no one would mind if I took a walk outside," she thought. But the men had arrived to put up the huge green-and-white striped canvas tent which covered a large part of the lawn, and she felt in the way.

She tried reading a magazine on the flagstone terrace, but even there the traffic was so heavy, with people moving chairs and rearranging furniture and carrying various boxes and packages, that she felt uncomfortable and went indoors.

"I guess my room is the only safe place to stay," she thought. "At least I won't bother anyone there. But it isn't how I thought I'd be spending my time—alone in my room."

The hours dragged until three o'clock. Suddenly there was a burst of noise downstairs. "Oh, I guess everyone's arrived for the rehearsal," she thought happily. "Now things will be more interesting." She straightened her skirt, made sure that her blouse was tucked in, and ran lightly down the steps.

"Here she is," said Bunny, who was surrounded by a crowd of young men and women. "I was just going upstairs to get you. Donna, meet my friends—Joan and Lucille and Johnny and Mike and Hal and Vince. This is Donna Parker, who was at Camp Cherrydale with me last summer. By the way, where's Ellie?"

Donna acknowledged the introductions with a shy, "How do you do." She would never learn which name belonged to which person.

"Oh, here's Ellie," someone called. Apparently they all knew Bunny's cousin, who came in with a smile.

"Now, where's Frank?" one of the young men asked. "Bunny, you don't think the groom has run off, do you?"

Bunny dimpled. "He'd better not try!" Then, more seriously, she added, "He had to stop to pick up Craig Haviland at the station, and said he might be a few minutes late. He'll meet us out in the garden. Miss Boyle is there."

"Good old Miss Boyle," one of the girls said—Donna thought it was Joan. "What would a wedding in Nottingham be without Miss Boyle to run it?"

Donna found, however, that a supervisor was indispensible to the proceedings. Miss Boyle lined everyone up in front of the tall evergreens at the entrance to the formal garden. Donna peeped inside the archway, and found it just as Ellie had described. The evergreens formed four sides, almost like walls of a room, the sky formed the ceiling, and thick green grass made a carpet. Men were putting small potted evergreens on either side of the central brick path.

"Oh, it's simply beautiful!" Donna thought. "It looks as though it were just made for a wedding."

"Ushers first," Miss Boyle was saying. "Oh, you're the best man, aren't you, Vince?" She seemed to know everyone. "You come in the other entrance with Frank, and stand near the altar. Now where's the fourth usher?"

"Here they come—Frank and Craig," Bunny said. "Darling, please hurry," she called to one of the two men who was hurrying across the lawn.

Donna turned. Frank must be the taller. Of course! She had met him last summer, on the final day of camp, when Bunny had proudly introduced him as "my fiancé."

"You fellows know everyone except Donna, don't you?" Bunny asked. "Donna, this is Frank Wilcox, and Craig Haviland."

"Haven't we met before?" Frank asked.

"At camp last summer," Donna reminded him. To herself she thought, "Well, I guess I didn't make any impression on him, if he doesn't even remember where he saw me."

Craig Haviland also took her hand. She looked up at him. He wasn't as dashing as Frank, but he was very good looking. His dark hair and skin, and heavy eyebrows, reminded her a little bit of her father, but his eyes were a clear gray. "And he's certainly a lot younger than Daddy," she thought, smiling back at him. "He looks younger than Frank, too."

"Now, are the ushers ready?" Miss Boyle asked. "Two by two, shortest pair first. And remember, everyone *please* step out with your left foot. Usher at the left, turn to the left at the end of the aisle; usher at the right, turn right. Good!" as Craig and another young man walked through the archway and down the brick path.

"When they have gone past two rows of chairs, the next two ushers step out. You'll have to imagine that the chairs are already in place. Ready, now—together!" She clapped her hands smartly.

"Now, the first pair of bridesmaids. Ellie and Miss—Miss

—" she looked at Donna. "Donna," Ellie supplied. Miss Boyle smiled brightly.

"You don't begin until the second pair of ushers has gone past four rows of chairs," the woman instructed them. "At the front, Ellie turns and stands next to Hal, and Donna stands next to Craig. Ready—*left!*"

Her elbow almost touching Ellie's so that they stayed together, Donna walked slowly down the aisle and turned sharply to the left.

"Don't look so scared," Craig said softly, when she took her place by his side. "You're not the one who's getting married." He smiled encouragingly.

Donna nodded. Craig was right—everyone would be looking at the bride, not at her.

"Fine, fine," Miss Boyle said, after Bunny had taken her place next to Frank where the altar would be. "It's too bad your father and your sister couldn't be here today, Bunny dear, but I'm sure they know exactly what to do. Now for the recessional."

Donna looked around, then realized that Miss Boyle meant that they would practice walking out.

"Now you take my arm," Craig whispered, crooking his right elbow in her direction, when it was their turn.

Somehow, holding on to Craig made her feel much more comfortable. She knew he would warn her before she did anything wrong.

"Well, that was just fine!" he said as they walked out of the garden. "You act like an experienced bridesmaid."

"Oh, but I'm not!" Donna protested. Still, it was nice that Craig felt she had done well. Everyone else was so interested in talking, and checking plans, that they hardly seemed to know she was there.

"You don't live in Nottingham, do you, Miss Parker?" the young man was saying.

"Call me Donna," she said demurely. "No, I live in a town called Summerfield."

"Summerfield? Oh, yes—I've heard of it. Do you go to school there?"

Did he think that she went to boarding school, like Ellie? she wondered. "Yes," she answered. "But I'm graduating in June." Goodness, it sounded as though she were graduating from high school, instead of junior high. But he probably went to college. She couldn't explain now that she was only in ninth grade.

"Graduating!" He smiled down at her, his gray eyes crinkling under the dark brows. "It seems only yesterday

that I was graduating, myself." He leaned toward her, and
whispered, "I'm only a lowly freshman at college. Thank
goodness this year is finished; I'd hate to do it again!"

"I'm not even thinking about college," Donna answered.
Goodness, that part was true enough! "And I'm having
such a wonderful time now, being on so many committees,
and planning for the commencement."

She could tell he was interested in what she was saying.
"And I've just been chosen valedictorian, too."

"You have?" Craig was obviously impressed. "Why,
that's wonderful. I'll bet you can't wait till graduation. Will
it be at night, with a dance afterwards?"

"Well, it will be at night, but there won't be a dance."
Would he think she was too young to go to dances? "But
we had a wonderful spring dance, with the gym decorated
just gorgeously. That was when my parents were in India."

"India! Wow! You do lead an exciting life, don't you?"

If he only knew, Donna thought wryly. Summerfield was
such a sleepy little town. Nothing exciting ever happened
there, but she couldn't let him guess that.

"Here!" called Bunny gaily. "What are you two whispering about?" Everyone turned and looked at them.

"Come on, men," Frank said just then. "I've gotten

orders to take the males away, so that these chattering females can have their gab fest. You're all coming to my house, you know."

"Do we know!" exclaimed Vince, who Donna remembered was Frank's best man. "Would we forget the bachelor dinner? Let's go, fellows—tonight's the night we say farewell to my old college roommate, to this poor man who is leaving the gay life forever."

"He doesn't look too unhappy," countered Ellie, as Frank grinned. "Anyhow, we'll have just as good a time at *our* party, won't we, Bunny?"

"Oh, dear," said Joan to Lucille. "We'll have to run home and change. Bunny, did you want us about six?"

Bunny nodded, and the men and the two girls left.

"It's just a little party for the bridesmaids," Bunny explained to Donna as they walked into the house with Ellie. "You don't really have to change."

"Are all the men college friends of Frank's?" Donna asked.

Bunny nodded. "All except Craig. He's Frank's cousin, and even though he's several years younger, they've been very friendly. And since I'm having my cousin"—she looked at Ellie—"Frank thought he would ask Craig."

"Are they all staying at a hotel?" Donna asked.

"No, at Frank's house," said Ellie, who seemed to know all about it. "That is, all except Craig. He's coming back here to sleep."

How wonderful! Donna thought as they went upstairs. Maybe he would be back before they went to bed. She would love to ask him more about college. And he was so easy to talk to. He was the only one who had really seemed to notice her.

She looked at the few dresses she had brought. Why hadn't Bunny told her there would be a party tonight? She should really wear something off-the-shoulder, with a sweeping skirt—the kind of thing that the magazines pictured for an informal college dance.

Well, her striped cotton shirtwaist dress would have to do. She hadn't worn it since she had gone to that movie with Paul. Goodness, that seemed years ago.

Suddenly she remembered the ring. No one had commented on it, or even seemed to notice it. But suppose someone—for instance, Craig—should ask her about it? It would be much simpler to leave it here in the bedroom. She slipped it off, and put it in its little box in her suitcase.

Ellie was back at her exercises. What a bore! How could

you talk to a girl who kept practicing ballet steps all the time? Of course, she had to admit that dancing did do something for a person. Ellie seemed so poised.

Donna looked in the mirror with distaste. If only she didn't have this babyish hair-do! She pulled it back into a pony tail, the way she had worn it on Blue Jean Day. No, that only made her look more childish.

She twisted the pony tail. How about a knot? A—what was it called—a chignon? She ran to get her bobby pins.

There! The pins held very nicely. And it really did make her look years older.

Ellie stopped in the middle of a kneebend, and stared at her. "What did you do to all your pretty hair?" she asked.

Donna turned, and showed the chignon proudly. "Don't you like it this way?"

Ellie shook her head. "I liked it the other way better, Donna. It's terribly sophisticated this way, but somehow it's not right for you."

Donna turned back to the mirror. So she wasn't supposed to look sophisticated? Was she supposed to be the baby of the wedding party? Well, Craig would like it this way!

"I like it," she said aloud. "Are you going to get dressed, Ellie? It's almost six o'clock."

CHAPTER 18   *Bunny's Wedding*

The little clock on the table between the two beds said eight o'clock. Donna looked over at the other bed. Ellie's golden hair covered part of her face; she was obviously still sound asleep.

Donna threw back her covers, and tiptoed over to the window. It was a beautiful summer morning, still delightfully fresh and dewy. "Just the kind of day to be married on," Donna thought, perching on the window sill.

She looked over toward the bureau, on which she had laid the small initialed silver compact which Bunny had given each of the bridesmaids at the party last night. She wondered why she hadn't enjoyed the party more. Everyone else had seemed to be having a wonderful time.

Bunny's older sister Phyllis, who was to be matron of honor, had arrived just before dinner was served, and

240

everyone had greeted her with joyous cries. Maybe that was it—maybe it was because she was the only outsider that she had felt ill at ease. Of course, they had all tried to make conversation with her, but she could see that they were much more interested in each other, in comparing notes about mutual friends, and telling stories about school and holiday plans. She had answered all their questions politely, trying not to bore them, and she had even asked them about themselves.

And then, after dinner, Bunny had showed them her trousseau and her gifts—linens, and lingerie, and silver. Maybe she had felt uncomfortable because, among all those beautiful things, her simple glass bowl had looked so insignificant. At the store it had seemed just right. Of course, Bunny had said she adored it, and all that, but it did look so awfully plain.

And maybe the thing that had spoiled the party was something Mrs. Knight had said. Donna tried to recall the words: "Bunny said she could just picture Donna and Ellie coming down the aisle together, Ellie so fair with her long blond hair, and Donna so dark, with her lovely dark hair *in that soft page-boy style.*"

Everyone had looked at her, and she had had a picture

of herself in the tight chignon. Well, there was nothing wrong with wearing it that way one night, certainly. Of course if Bunny wanted her to wear it loose at the wedding, she would do it. The headband of pink flowers would make it look a little better, anyhow. But why did they think they had to be so *tactful?* It had made her feel younger than ever, and more alone.

Donna's attention was caught by a movement below. Someone was carrying a breakfast tray out to the flagstone terrace beneath her. Why, it was Craig! She had been so disappointed that she had not seen him last night, but now there was a chance to talk to him again. What a lovely beginning for the day!

She glanced at Ellie, whose arm protected her eyes from the morning light. She would probably begin doing those silly exercises the minute she got up. And Bunny had said that Lucy would have breakfast ready whenever they wanted it. If she hurried, she would be able to carry her tray out to the terrace, too.

"Well, if it isn't the lady from Summerfield!" Craig said, rising from his chair as she approached him. "It looks as though we're the only early birds around. The bride's probably catching up on her beauty sleep. I hope your party didn't last as late as ours did."

It was so easy to carry on a conversation with Craig. He made her feel grownup, and sure of herself. She found herself telling him more about her parents' trip to India, and her own trip to California.

"I'd love to hear more about it," he said as they finished breakfast, "but I guess we'd better go inside now. Things seem to be stirring."

Donna recalled the wording on the invitation. The wedding was to be at noon, followed by a wedding breakfast. Luckily her mother had told her that a "wedding breakfast" was really a luncheon, and usually a fancy one at that. She had had ideas of bacon and eggs, which seemed terribly ordinary.

"There isn't much time," she agreed. "But everything seems to be getting done somehow. Let's not go in just yet."

What could she do, back in her own bedroom? Sit and wait until Ellie decided to wake up? She tossed her head. She would show everyone that she was just as grown-up and important as they were. Wasn't she having breakfast with a real, honest-to-goodness college man? But how could she keep him from leaving her alone?

"Oh, look!" she cried. "Here come the flowers. Aren't

they absolutely gorgeous? Where are they going to put all of them?"

"At the altar, I guess, and inside the tent, and on the tables," Craig answered.

"Let's see what the formal garden looks like," Donna said, catching Craig's hand and playfully pulling him up from his chair. "You know, a gentleman mustn't refuse a lady."

Craig smiled. "Well, we'll have to hurry. But you're right—it wouldn't be nice to refuse."

Donna linked her arm through Craig's, as they walked across the lawn to the evergreen enclosure. Miss Boyle was already there, supervising some men who were connecting the small evergreens lining the central brick path with two rolls of wide white satin ribbon. The chairs were already in place, and at the far end of the enclosure white flowers were banked about the altar.

"How lovely!" Donna sighed.

Miss Boyle looked up. "Good morning," she said cheerfully. "Yes, everything has worked out so well. I'm sure the Knights will be pleased." She looked at her watch. "Oh, dear, the time goes so quickly. Before we know it, the guests will be arriving."

"I suppose we'd better go back," Donna said, rather hoping that Craig would contradict her. Instead, he nodded and started toward the house.

"Well!" Ellie was brushing her hair as Donna entered the bedroom. "What worm was this little early bird out after? Oh, don't think I didn't see you walking with Craig." She pointed her brush playfully at Donna.

Donna's mouth opened, then closed. Maybe Ellie hadn't meant the remark the way it sounded. Certainly there had been nothing wrong with having breakfast with Craig. It was Ellie's own fault that she had slept late, and would have to hurry now.

"Miss Boyle thinks we ought to be getting dressed," Donna said, changing the subject. She took her new dyed slippers out of the closet. Just then there was a knock at the bedroom door, and Ellie went to get the white boxes which Lucy held.

"Oh, our flowers!" Donna said, as Ellie brought out two small bands made of pink roses and sweetpeas, and two cascades of the same flowers, trimmed with pink satin ribbon.

"Miss Bunny said she'd like to see both of you when you're all dressed," announced Lucy, who was as interested in the contents of the boxes as the girls.

"And I want to see her," Donna thought as she pinned the flowers in her dark hair. "I'll bet she looks gorgeous."

But she was hardly prepared for the sight which met her eyes as they entered Bunny's room. She could only gasp.

"Do I look all right?" Bunny asked, although her smile showed that she knew the answer. Donna nodded, silently admiring the gown of embroidered white organdy, the short white veil, the magnificent cascade of white flowers, and most of all the radiant beauty of the bride.

"You both look sweet," the girl in white said, as Ellie and Donna turned and pirouetted gracefully for her approval. "Oh, dear, how will I be able to wait until noon?"

From the sounds below, Donna could tell that the guests were arriving. The ushers were probably out there now, politely murmuring "Friend of the bride, or friend of the groom?"

The other bridesmaids, and Bunny's sister, appeared in a few moments. They all looked, Donna thought, like pictures from a bride's magazine. Everything was so perfect— she hoped she would do nothing to spoil it. Suppose she tripped and fell while walking down the aisle? What if she suddenly got a coughing spell?

It was with a sigh of relief, a little while later, that she took her place at the front of the garden next to Craig. The procession had gone smoothly, and with Craig to help her walk out, she had nothing to worry about. She smiled happily at him, and he smiled back.

Donna watched the ceremony with interest, and in all too short a time was standing outside the garden. What had Miss Boyle said about the receiving line? Yes, there was Mrs. Knight, Mr. Wilcox, Mrs. Wilcox, Mr. Knight, and then Bunny standing next to Frank. Well, she would just stay with Craig and do whatever he did.

"Donna," Ellie motioned, "come over here." Donna turned to the young man at her side. What was wrong with standing beside him?

"The ushers aren't part of the receiving line," Ellie said in a low voice. "You stay here with the bridesmaids."

Donna took her place as Mrs. Knight began receiving the guests. So many strange faces! And she had to shake hands with each one of them, and smile, and say "I'm Donna Parker, a friend of Bunny's. How do you do?"

People were strolling over to the tent—Mrs. Knight called it a "marquee"—and she wondered whether Craig had joined them. The line of guests seemed to go on forever, and she heaved a sigh of relief when Mrs. Knight finally turned and said, "Well, everyone seems to have been greeted. I think we can leave now. Thank you so much for helping."

"Doesn't it look gorgeous?" Donna said to Ellie when they reached the marquee. "I never thought they'd be able to lay a whole dance floor here, and still have room for so many tables."

The decorators had indeed done a magnificent job. Small circular tables, each seating six people, were covered with pink tablecloths, and a long table for the bridal party occupied one end of the enclosure. A lavish buffet had been laid on another long table, with beautifully decorated salads, cold sliced meats, and casseroles containing hot dishes.

But it was the floral arrangements which were most impressive. On each table was a low centerpiece of pink flowers. All the poles which held up the tent were transformed into dogwood trees, with branches of pink blossoms and greens. In each corner of the marquee were massed evergreens, and the musicians' platform was screened by a miniature picket fence covered with greens and pink flowers.

The guests were helping themselves to food from the

buffet, then seating themselves at the small tables.

"Should we get our plates now?" Donna asked Ellie.

Ellie shook her head, and guided Donna across the room to the bridal table. "The people in the bridal party are always served by waiters," she explained.

"Gee," Donna thought with an uncomfortable feeling. "She must think I'm awfully stupid."

"Here," Ellie said, "we'll keep a place between us for one of the ushers. They'll be here in a minute."

To Donna's delight and relief, it was Craig who sat next to her. "Isn't it a lovely wedding?" she asked.

"Vince had better hurry and toast the bride," Craig was saying. "I'm starved."

Donna suddenly discovered that she too was hungry. "Oh, this food is just yummy," she said. "I think this is one of the nicest weddings I've ever been to." And the only one, she thought to herself, but she was sure no one would ever know that. "Don't you agree, Craig?"

Craig nodded, but Donna gave him no chance to speak. She had a feeling that as long as she kept talking, everything would be all right.

"It certainly seems funny to be among all these people, and not know any of them," she went on. "Oh," she said hastily, "I don't mean you, Craig, or Bunny, or—or Ellie. I mean all the *guests*. Because in Summerfield I know just about everybody. Of course, it's a small town, but it's so *friendly*. After all, I grew up there, and everybody knows the Parkers."

Craig was listening, but Ellie kept her eyes fixed on her plate. What could be so fascinating about the food? Ellie was a strange sort of girl.

"And it's close to New York, too, you know," she went on. "Why we go in quite often. Just a few weeks ago my mother took a friend of mine, and me, to see the ballet. It was terribly interesting."

At the mention of ballet, Ellie looked up. *Oh, dear,* Donna thought. *Why did I mention that? Now she'll begin to talk about her ballet school, and I don't feel at all like hearing about that!*

"Oh, look, Craig!" she cried. "Bunny's going to cut the cake!" For the bride had picked up a silver cake knife, the handle decorated with pink flowers to match the table centerpiece. Frank stood up with her, and placed his right hand over hers.

Suddenly, someone began to sing "The bride cuts the cake," to the tune of "The Farmer in the Dell," and everyone joined in. There was applause as they finished, and a photographer's flash camera caught their happy smiles.

The orchestra, which until now had been playing soft background music, broke into a gay waltz, and everyone watched as Frank led Bunny in the first dance. Then Mr. Knight danced with his daughter, and Frank danced with Mrs. Knight. Donna watched the ever-widening circle of dancers, as the guests began to join the wedding party on the floor, and finally the moment she had been waiting for arrived.

"May I have this dance?" Craig asked very formally.

He asked me before he asked Ellie, Donna thought. But they had gone only a few steps when one of the other ushers cut in. Then the guests, young men and older ones, each seemed to feel called upon to dance with her.

"I don't even know who they are," Donna thought despairingly, "and frankly I'm not very much interested. And most of them are such queer dancers I can't even follow them, and they keep stepping on my toes. I wish they'd let me dance with Craig."

The music ended, and the stout gray-haired man who was her partner started to lead her back to her table, which was now deserted. She had a sudden vision of herself sitting at the long board, entirely alone, with everyone whispering about her.

She turned to her escort. "If you'll excuse me," she said, "I have to go back to the house for a minute. I—I need my handkerchief."

The man smiled, and let her go. She slipped along the wall of the marquee, trying not to attract attention. But just as she reached a corner where a number of potted evergreens were grouped tightly together, the music began, and she found herself wedged in and surrounded by dancers.

And here came Craig, dancing with Ellie. She couldn't let them see her in this position. Making herself as small as possible, she disappeared behind the evergreens. But Ellie and Craig seemed to have stopped a few feet away.

". . . and has she told you about her trip to California yet?" she heard Ellie say. Good heavens, was she talking about *her*? Donna stood motionless.

"Yes, and about her parents' trip to India, too," the young man's voice answered. "But I don't know why that should annoy you, Ellie."

"And the way she's gone after you, Craig. Running out to have breakfast with you this morning, and putting her hair up that silly way last night so you'd think she was older, and hardly letting you out of her sight. Doesn't she realize how it looks to other people? In a way I blame you, Craig. Why didn't you tell her that she was making a fool of herself?"

Donna found herself shaking. What a dreadful girl that Ellie Townsend was! Craig would certainly tell her a thing or two. She hoped they didn't move away before she heard his answer.

Craig, it seemed, had stopped dancing entirely. She could tell from his voice that he had led Ellie away from the dance floor, closer to the corner where she was standing. Suppose they saw her now! She shrank further back against the evergreens.

"Now listen here, my fair young lady," Craig was saying. "I think you should be ashamed of yourself."

There! she thought. She knew he would.

"Don't you understand," he continued, "how lonely and uncomfortable that poor kid feels? Anyone can tell she's been stuck in that little town all her life. She certainly doesn't fly around the country the way you do from Olympia to New York. That California trip is a big thing to her."

Donna chewed nervously at a fingernail. This wasn't at all what Craig should be saying.

"And she doesn't know a soul here, except Bunny, who's too busy to pay much attention to her. Certainly I realize she's trying to act more grown-up than she is, and that some of the things she's done may seem pretty silly to you. But I feel that it's little enough for me to do, to talk to her and try to make her feel that someone is interested in her. She's alone, and bewildered, and I feel sorry for her."

Oh! Donna put her hand over her mouth so that she would not cry out. The voices of Craig and Ellie drifted away, and Donna darted out and through the open doorway of the tent.

She flew toward the house, the tears now streaming down her cheeks. *The way she's run after you, Craig! Making a fool of herself!*

She raced up the stairs and toward her bedroom. *Stuck in that little town all her life! I feel awfully sorry for her!*

She looked wildly about her. Why wasn't she in her own bedroom, in her own nice safe house? Why had she ever come here, to be humiliated in this way? How could she ever face Craig, or Ellie, or even the Knights, knowing what they must think of her?

She opened her suitcase, and began throwing her things into it. She couldn't stay here another minute!

CHAPTER 19   *Donna Runs Away*

"Oh, pardon me, dear, I didn't know anyone was in here." Mrs. Knight stood at the door of the bedroom. She looked at the girl in her traveling clothes, suitcase in hand.

"Th-that's all right," Donna answered. She hoped the cold water had removed the redness from her eyes, but she found it difficult to keep her voice steady. "I—I was just going to look for you, to say good-by."

"Is something wrong, dear?" The older woman seemed concerned. "Aren't you coming down to watch the bride toss her bouquet?"

"I have to—to go home," Donna said, rolling her damp handkerchief into a ball. "Please give Bunny my regrets, and tell her I'm sorry I had to leave so early. I—I hope she won't mind."

Mrs. Knight hesitated. "Of course you know best, dear.

We'd love to have you stay, but we certainly don't want to insist, if you feel you must leave. And I'm sure Bunny will understand. One of the ushers will drive you to the station."

"Oh, no!" Donna protested. Suppose Craig were to volunteer to take her there? "I've called a cab already, and the man said it would be here in a few minutes." She twisted her handkerchief. "Thank you very much for inviting me. I'd better go now." She picked up her suitcase.

Wasn't I lucky that everyone was outside in the tent? she thought as she slipped out the front door and into the waiting cab. She had seen in the hall mirror that her eyes were still swollen.

"There's a train to New York in about fifteen minutes, miss," the driver said, as she paid him at the station. "Wait right here, and you can't miss it."

The train ride seemed to take forever. Donna kept her face turned away from the other passengers, and looked intently out of the window. The trip up here had been so different. Who ever would have thought that things would have turned out this way, that she would actually be running away from Bunny's wedding?

But she never could have faced the people there. Did

they all feel about her the way Ellie and Craig did? *Doesn't she realize how it looks to other people?* Ellie had said that, so probably everyone was laughing at her, or was annoyed by her behavior. *Some of the things she's done may seem pretty silly,* Craig had replied.

What had ever possessed her to act that way? She was the girl who had wanted to leave the bowling alley a few weeks ago, because she had been afraid the boys might think she was looking at them. She was the one who had thought it wrong for Karen to ask Tommy to carry her books. She, Donna Parker, was the girl who had refused to smile at Paul, that day she had not recognized him on the path outside the school, because she wouldn't say hello to someone she didn't know! And then she was the person who had run after Craig so that everyone was talking about it!

"And I was so sure I'd never do something I'd be ashamed of," she thought sadly, as she picked up her bag to change trains in New York City. "What happened to me?"

All the way to Summerfield she kept musing over the question, and she was still worrying about it when she alighted from the train, and went to call her parents on the telephone inside the little station.

"Donna!" Mrs. Parker exclaimed, on hearing her daughter's voice. "You're here in Summerfield? Why, we hadn't expected you home for hours and hours. Is something wrong? Yes, of course we'll come and get you immediately."

"Oh, I'm all right," Donna answered a little while later, seated in the back seat of the Parker car with Jimmy. "I thought I'd better not get home too late. Yes, it was a beautiful wedding."

Mr. Parker took his eyes from the road long enough to give his wife a quizzical glance. His wife looked back with an expression that, if Donna had seen it, she would have translated as, "Yes, I realize that something is wrong, but this is not the time for further questions. Just let me handle it in my own way."

"I guess I'll unpack," Donna said as she went up the stairs to her room. "Will you have time to listen to me say the valedictory before dinner, Mommy?"

"I'll be upstairs in a minute, Cooky," Mrs. Parker said. "Be sure to change your clothes."

Donna had just hung the limp organdy dress in the closet, and put away the dyed slippers, when Mrs. Parker appeared at the door.

"Oh, I'm not finished yet, Mommy," Donna said.

"That's all right, dear." Mrs. Parker came into the room, closed the door behind her, and sat down on the edge of Donna's bed. "Would you like to tell me about the wedding now? I'm very much interested."

Donna sat down on the other side of the bed. "Well, let's see. The Knights have a lovely house, and the grounds around it are simply gorgeous, Mommy. Bunny was married out in the garden, and then the reception was held in this perfectly huge tent, with an orchestra and a dance floor and everything."

Suddenly she saw herself cowering behind the evergreens in the corner, and listening to the conversation between Ellie and Craig. Her lower lip began to quiver.

"What's the matter, dear?" her mother asked. "What happened?"

Donna put her head down on the bed and started to sob. "Oh, Mommy," she said through her tears. "It was just awful. I felt so uncomfortable, and everyone was strange, and—and—I made a fool of myself!"

Mrs. Parker patted her daughter's shoulder. "Oh, honey, I'm so sorry. What did you do?"

Donna sat up and wiped her eyes. "Oh, I tried to act

older than I really am, and I guess I bragged about going
to California. And—and Ellie—she's Bunny's cousin—
Ellie said I ran after one of the ushers, and acted silly. But,
Mommy"—she started to sniffle again—"Mommy, I didn't
realize that I was acting that way. Why did I do it?"

Mrs. Parker sighed. "Why do lots of us do foolish things
sometimes? You were alone, and probably frightened."

"But I've been alone before, Mommy. When you and
Daddy went to India I was alone for six weeks."

"Not really, dear. You were in your own house, and had
your friends around you, and someone here to take care of
you. But in Nottingham it was different. You acted that
way because you felt insecure."

"What do you mean, insecure?"

"You lost your feeling of safety, of being protected and
cared for. And that's a very important thing to almost all
of us. When people lose their sense of security, they feel
that the whole world has turned against them, and they
have to fight. I know another girl who is fighting back by
putting on airs and doing almost exactly what you did."

Donna stopped in the middle of a sob. "Another girl?"
Her eyes opened wide. "Why, Ricky! Was I really that
bad? Oh, my goodness!"

Then she shook her head. "But, Mommy, she still has her father, and her friends, and her own house." Then she changed her mind. "No, I guess everything does look different to Ricky now. I guess she really does feel all alone. And I haven't been very nice to her, have I?"

Mrs. Parker stood up. "Donna dear, just remember that growing up isn't all fun. And this wasn't a completely bad experience."

"Well, I wish it hadn't happened. I wish I hadn't gone."

Mrs. Parker paused, her hand on the doorknob. "You can't be sheltered all your life, dear. I realize that it takes courage to face new situations, but I hope you have it."

"You mean you're glad that this happened?" Donna asked in a shocked tone.

"Not the way you mean it, Cooky. I'm only glad if you learned something from it. What happens to us is not nearly so important as what we do with the knowledge gained."

"Goodness!" Donna thought when she was alone in the room, and had started to change her clothes. "My mother can turn almost anything into a lecture. What am I supposed to have learned from this weekend?"

She picked up her comb. "In a way, maybe Mommy's right. I guess I did feel insecure, like Ricky. I wonder whether boys ever feel that way."

She pulled at a tangle in her hair. "Paul!" she suddenly thought. "Why, that's what's the matter with him. I guess when his father was out of work he felt insecure too. And then his mother started working and it made things worse, and *his* whole world looked different. So he fought back by leaving school and going to work."

"Are you ready with your speech?" Mrs. Parker called.

"In a minute, Mommy." Well, now that she had found out why Ricky and Paul acted the way they did, what was she supposed to do about it? She certainly couldn't make Ricky change, or Paul either.

"May I invite Ricky over for supper, Mommy?" she asked as she came downstairs, speech in hand.

Mrs. Parker looked pleased. "That's a lovely idea."

"Goodness!" Donna thought. "Now Mommy will feel that I'm being nice to Ricky because of the wedding. And it's only because I'd like to talk to her."

"Thanks for asking me," Ricky said after they had finished supper, and gone up to Donna's bedroom. "Father had to work this weekend, and I was getting so bored."

Donna nodded. Poor Ricky, all alone in that house. Then she stopped short. The worst thing in the world was to feel sorry for Ricky. She could hear Craig's voice: *I feel so sorry for her.* That had been the final blow.

"Well," she said, "Monday graduation practice begins, and that'll be exciting."

"Not for me," Ricky replied, turning the pages of an old magazine, and not looking at her friend. "I can't wait till graduation is over."

Is she going to begin to talk about Europe again? Donna wondered.

But it was graduation night itself that concerned Ricky.

"Everyone else will go there with their mothers and fathers," Ricky said. "But my—my mother—won't be there. I'll see all the other mothers in the audience, looking so happy, and watching us come down the aisle and get our diplomas on the stage. And I'll be remembering her every minute." She turned toward her friend. "Oh, Donna," she whispered, "how will I be able to stand it?"

"You mustn't think about it," the dark-haired girl said. "Your father will be there, and he'll be awfully proud of you. Just think how pleased he'll be when you get the Outstanding Girl award." Gracious, what was she saying? She had been complaining about Ricky and the award all this time, and now she was telling her she would win it.

"Oh, Donna, do you really think I'll get it?" Ricky closed the magazine. "I couldn't bear a summer here in Summerfield, and if I do get the prize, I know Daddy would keep his word and take me to Europe. And I've got to get away from here."

Donna nodded. Of course she had to. She had to leave and make a fresh start. Think how terrible it would have been, Donna thought, if she had had to stay in Nottingham. She never would have gotten over a little thing like the wedding.

"Oh, I know you'll win the prize," Donna repeated. "You've just got to!" To her surprise, she found that she meant it. All she herself really wanted was all *A*'s, she thought, so she could go to California. She would much rather have Ricky win the award.

"Is your dress ready?" Ricky asked. "Are you still going to wear the one your Uncle Roger gave you for your birthday? It's so pretty."

"But yours is new." Wasn't Ricky pleased with the dress?

"I sent it back," Ricky admitted. "It looked all right in New York, but not when I tried it on at home."

Donna breathed a sigh of relief. "Did you get another dress, Ricky? There are still lots of pretty ones here."

"Not yet. Would—" the girl hesitated, "would you come with me to look for one after school?"

"I'd love to," was the enthusiastic answer.

"Donna," Mrs. Parker called from the top of the stairs. "Would Ricky like Daddy to drive her home now? He wants to get a newspaper at the store."

Ricky stood up. "I'll see you at school, Donna. Gee, you hardly said a thing about the wedding. Remember to tell me about it."

Donna finished unpacking her suitcase and putting away her clothes after Ricky had left. She ran her hand inside the compartment at the side of the case, to make sure she had taken everything out, and found a little box tucked in a corner.

"Paul's ring!" she realized suddenly. "I'd completely forgotten about it." She opened the box and looked at the silver band, remembering the boy who had run all the way to the station to give it to her. Should she wear it, or should she return it? She hadn't even told her parents about it.

"I'll decide on Monday," she resolved. "It looks as though that's going to be the three R's day. And I don't mean Reading, 'Riting and 'Rithmetic, either. Monday will be Ring, Rehearsals, and"—she crossed her fingers—"Reports!"

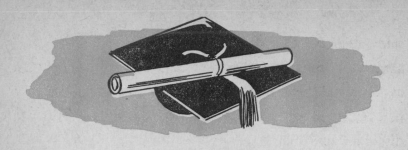

CHAPTER 20   *Graduation Night*

Donna dragged her feet up the front steps of her house, and sat down on one of the chairs that her father had put on the porch a few days before. In her hand she held a small brown envelope. If only she didn't have to go in and face her mother!

The morning had started so beautifully. It was so much fun to be in school and not have any classes. The auditorium had been filled with ninth-graders, and as soon as she entered she had been surrounded by Joyce and Anne and Karen, wanting to know all the details about the wedding. Luckily, she had only a few minutes to describe the Knight's house when Mr. Greer had called for order.

Then there had been all the excitement of lining up, and marching down the two long aisles, and taking their places on the tiers of seats which had been set up on the stage. And Mr. Oldenburg had led them in the pledge of allegiance, which somehow sounded much more stirring as they stood there facing the empty auditorium. Then they had had to practice walking across the stage to get their diplomas, and marching out again.

And when it was over, everyone else had gone to the office to get report cards, but she had had to stay with Miss Griffith to rehearse her valedictory. It had been fun to listen to George Hart give his speech of welcome, even though she wanted so badly to finish and learn what marks she had been given. And then George had left, and she had stood alone on the stage, while Miss Griffith stopped her whenever she spoke too quickly, or ran her words together. And then, when Miss Griffith was satisfied, and dismissed her, she had hurried all the way to the office.

"You're the very last one," the secretary had said with a smile. "But I peeked, and you have a lovely report, Donna."

"I do?" Her heart began to pound rapidly, and her fingers fumbled so that she had trouble getting the white card out of its envelope.

"Oh!" She muffled a cry. There were all those pretty triangular *A*'s for English and Latin, history and science.

But Donna hardly saw them. For there, at the bottom of the list, and next to the word *algebra,* stood a big, ugly *B!*

Slowly Donna put the card back into the envelope. Slowly she walked out of the office, and slowly she went home. It wasn't fair! She had worked so hard. And now, because of one mark—because of one exam, really—she would miss a whole trip to California. If only her father hadn't said what he did to Uncle Roger about her studying. If only Uncle Roger hadn't taken him seriously! If only she hadn't been so sure that she could get all *A*'s!

The front door opened, and Mrs. Parker came out on the porch. "I thought I heard someone come up the steps, Donna. Why are you sitting out here?" She noticed the envelope in Donna's hand. "Why, dear, you've gotten your report." She put out her hand, but Donna held on to the card for a moment.

"Mommy—" She swallowed hard. "I did work hard; really I did. Please remember that."

Mrs. Parker looked at the report card, then turned to her daughter. "Why, Donna, that's a perfectly beautiful report!"

Was her mother serious? "But I got a *B* in algebra, Mommy." Hadn't she seen that?

"I know, Cooky. But it still is a fine report, and I'm proud of you. Oh—" as Donna started to interrupt, "I know you wanted all *A*'s, but you mustn't let a little thing like that upset you." She paused. "I think I hear the telephone ringing. Now don't sit out here and brood, Donna."

A little thing, Donna thought! How could her mother say that losing a trip to California was a "little thing"?

"It's for you, Donna!" Mrs. Parker called.

"Oh, hi, Ricky," Donna said when she heard the other girl's voice. "Yes, I guess it'll be all right to go shopping for your dress in a little while. My report? Oh, it was all right, I guess. You did?" She gulped. "You got all *A*'s? Really? Gee, that's swell." Ricky sounded so happy.

She hung up. "If Ricky could do it," she said to her mother, "why couldn't I?"

"Donna!" Mrs. Parker said sharply. "Now stop that! Surely you're not going to let one mark ruin your whole graduation." Then she smiled. "Come on, Cooky. Let's see a shining face. This is supposed to be a happy time, and I'd hate to see you spoil it."

Donna was halfway up the steps when she turned around and went back to the kitchen.

"I almost forgot to give you the tickets for graduation,

Mommy. There's one for you, and one for Daddy, and one for Jimmy. And one extra for anyone who wants it." She thumbtacked the tickets to the bulletin board. "And Joyce is having a party after graduation. May I go?"

Mrs. Parker nodded. "Of course, dear."

"That must be Ricky," Donna said at the sound of footsteps on the front porch. But when she answered the ringing of the doorbell, she found that it was not Ricky.

"Paul!" she exclaimed in surprise. "What are you doing here in the middle of the day? Aren't you working?"

"Can you come and sit out on the porch for a minute, Donna?" the boy asked anxiously. "I'd like to talk to you."

Now what? Donna thought. *Hasn't enough gone wrong today?*

"I'm not working any more, Donna," Paul said. Heavens! Had he lost his job, too?

Then he smiled. "I know what you're thinking. No, I wasn't fired. I left because I'm going to summer school."

"Paul! How wonderful! Will you be able to go back to school in September?"

He nodded. "My father has a new position, Donna. And I hate to admit this, but I guess he was right. It's a much better job than his other one, and it's right here in Summerfield, with very little traveling."

That must be the one Daddy was talking about, Donna thought. Aloud she said, "Will your mother stop working?"

The boy frowned. "That's the first thing I thought of too, Donna." He rubbed his jaw. "But when I asked her, she said she wouldn't dream of stopping—that she was having loads of fun. Gee, it certainly didn't sound that way to me. I thought she was working because we needed the money."

"Then why did she complain about all the trouble she was having, Paul? Did you ask her that?"

"She just laughed, and said she didn't think it had sounded like complaining. She even said she thought I would be interested in the stories she was telling us." Paul looked at her, a puzzled expression in his eyes. "Gee, Donna, do you think she really likes working, instead of staying home?"

"It sounds that way," Donna said. But to herself she thought, "Poor Paul. When your world is turned upside down, you certainly do funny things. You hear what you want to hear, and you believe what you want to believe."

Well, maybe her mother was right. Bunny's wedding had been awful to live through, but at least she could understand Paul and Ricky a little better now.

She looked at the boy sitting beside her. "Will you have to go to school all summer, Paul?"

"It's only six weeks. And it starts earlier this year—it runs from the middle of June till the end of July. I thought maybe I'd see whether I could go back to Camp Three Pines for August, if they still want me."

"Oh, that would be wonderful! I'm going to Cherry-dale for August, you know." And since Paul would be home for July, too, maybe she wouldn't miss not having the California trip quite so much.

She looked down at her hands. Had Paul noticed that she wasn't wearing his ring? What should she do? She didn't want to hurt his feelings. On the other hand, she didn't ever again want to feel that she was putting on airs, or acting too grown-up. She would really feel much better if he took it back.

She stood up. "Would you wait here a minute, Paul? I want to get something."

When she returned, she had something in each hand. "I—I don't think I'd better wear this now, Paul. It was awfully nice of you to think of me, though, and I would like us to be friends." She handed him the little box.

Before he could speak, she held out the white card which

was in her other hand. "This is a ticket for graduation night. I only have one extra one. Would you like to come?"

He took the ticket. "Gee, thanks, Donna. I'd love to see the graduation. Golly, it seems only yesterday that I was up there on the stage myself. Thanks a lot."

Well, maybe graduation wouldn't be so bad after all, Donna thought as she watched him leave. And her excitement continued to mount as she went shopping with Ricky and they selected a charming organdy dress with a full skirt. "It reminds me a little of my bridesmaid's dress," Donna thought. "I only hope that graduation night is happier than that weekend was."

At least there was nothing wrong with her dress, she decided as she turned around for her parents' inspection on the eventful evening. Even Jimmy whistled.

"Why can't I escort this lovely young lady to her graduation exercises?" Mr. Parker said admiringly.

"Oh, Daddy," Donna giggled. "I'm not leaving forever, just because I have to be at school before you do. And I'll meet you as soon as it's over."

And the procession down the aisle was most impressive, she could tell from the admiring glances of the audience as she mounted the steps to the stage.

And her speech was fine, because even though her throat was a little dry and the palms of her hands a little moist, she knew from her mother's smile, and her father's "prize-fighter" handshake, that she had done well.

Now only the awards remained to be given. She could feel the glances around her when Mr. Greer spoke of the Outstanding Boy and Outstanding Girl prizes. Of course George Hart won the boy's award.

"And for the outstanding girl," Mr. Greer announced, "we have chosen a young lady who is not only at the top of her class in scholarship, and has been a leader in many school and class activities, but also a girl who can serve as an example to all of us for her friendliness, her perseverance, and her courage. I take great pleasure in presenting this award to—Miss Fredericka West!"

There was a moment's hush, and then applause as Ricky, her face almost as red as her hair, came forward.

Donna saw Ricky look into the faces of the audience for her father, and when Ricky smiled at him, Donna smiled too. "Oh, I'm so glad," Donna whispered to the girl next to her. "Ricky really deserved it."

"Deserved it!" Anne and Karen practically shrieked after they had marched out of the auditorium.

7

"What did Mr. Greer say about her friendliness?" Karen said. "I could tell him a couple of things."

"Oh, Karen, you shouldn't say that," Donna protested. "Ricky really wasn't so bad. And I honestly don't mind not winning the award, especially when it meant so much to her. The only thing I minded," she added wistfully, "was not getting an *A* in algebra."

"Gee, Donna," Joyce said. "I feel terrible about that. I should have helped you more. It was my fault."

"Joyce! Of course it wasn't anyone's fault but my own! And I shouldn't have counted so much on getting all *A*'s."

"Donna!" Mrs. Parker, coming up to the girls with her husband and Jimmy, took her daughter's arm. "This came for you after you left." She held out a telegram. "I have an idea it's from Uncle Roger."

Donna took the envelope and sighed. "I guess he wants to send his best wishes. Well, it was nice of him to think of me. But, oh"—her lips trembled as she ripped open the flap— "I can't help thinking that a ticket would have been much more exciting than a telegram."

The girls crowded around her. Donna's eyes ran quickly across the words. Then she gasped, and her naturally rosy cheeks became even rosier. "Oh, no!" she murmured.

"What is it, Donna?" Mrs. Parker asked.

But Donna was rereading the message. "Here!" she said weakly, holding the paper out to her mother. "I don't think I know what I'm reading."

Joyce, Karen, and Anne had moved back silently. They looked at Donna, who in turn was watching her mother. Mr. Parker had come over to stand beside his wife.

> Congratulations wonderful report. Will swap
> B in algebra for valedictory. Ticket following.
> Love Aunt Adele and Uncle Roger.

Mrs. Parker looked at her husband and smiled happily. "Oh, Sam, I'm so glad. I was sure that Roger wanted Donna to get all A's only to satisfy you. Did you get it straightened out with him, dear?"

Mr. Parker nodded and grinned. "I certainly did, honey. I also told him how hard she had worked, and how proud we were of her for being chosen valedictorian. After all, a B is nothing to be ashamed of, either. The only reason Roger told Donna that she'd have to get all A's was because of what I said you know, about her concentrating on the trip and not studying." He put an arm around Donna's waist. "But goodness knows I'm pleased, so I guess Roger is, too."

Donna's thoughts were racing. That day of Uncle Roger's visit, what had her father said? "See what you've done? Do you think she'll get one minute's worth of studying now?"

And what had Uncle Roger answered? "You mean if she does poorly at school it will be my fault?" Well, no one could say she had done poorly!

"Oh, Daddy! And I was so disappointed that I hadn't gotten all *A*'s. Why didn't you tell me that I could go to California anyhow?"

Mr. Parker looked down at his daughter, his expression quite serious. "Sweetie, frankly I didn't know. Uncle Roger had made the bargain with you, and it was up to him to change it, if he wanted to." Then his eyes twinkled. "And if you hadn't been working for all *A*'s, goodness knows what that report would have looked like!"

Donna stood quite still. Maybe her father was right. Maybe you had to aim just a little higher than you were supposed to go.

"Are you really going to California?" Joyce asked, her eyes shining. "And I don't have to feel badly about your algebra any more?"

Donna snapped her fingers. "Goodness, here I stand

dreaming." She flung her arms around Joyce's neck. "No, you don't have to worry one more minute—not that you ever should have, Joyce. And you know, you were the one who told me to write the valedictory, so I have you to thank for the trip anyhow. Oh, I'm going to California—really!"

Then she hugged her father, and her mother, and Jimmy, and Anne and Karen. "I'm going to California! I'm going to California!" she repeated.

"California, here I come . . ." the girls started to sing.

"What's going on?" asked a young male voice. The singing suddenly stopped.

"Oh, Paul," Donna said. "I'm so glad you could come tonight. You know everyone here, don't you?"

The boy nodded, and shook hands with the Parkers.

"I only wanted to thank you for inviting me, Donna. Your speech was great. And I wanted to tell you that, after summer school, I'll be going back to Three Pines."

"Well, I'll probably be in California while you're in summer school," Donna said, hardly able to believe the words even as she said them. "But I'm sure I'll see you at camp."

Ricky and Mr. West came up to join the group, as the others left with their parents, and Paul said good-by.

"We'll see you at the party, Joyce," Donna called, as she went over to Ricky.

"Aren't you proud of your daughter?" Mrs. Parker said to Mr. West. "It's quite an honor, winning the award."

"Indeed I am," Mr. West said. "And I'm sure you're proud of Donna, too. We have two Outstanding Girls, don't we?" He looked at his red-haired daughter, and dark-haired Donna standing next to her. "And now we're off for sights unknown. I think my little girl deserves a very special kind of vacation."

"We'll take Ricky and Donna to Joyce's house," Mr. Parker offered.

"And could I call you when we're ready to come home, Father?" Ricky asked. Mr. West nodded, beaming. They all walked out together.

Donna looked back at the building, still ablaze at this late hour. She took a deep breath of the balmy night air. The end of Summerfield Junior High! In the fall, when she came back, it would be to senior high school.

"I know why some people call tonight graduation, and some people call it commencement," she said to Ricky, as they walked toward the Parkers' car. "It's the end of some things. But it's the beginning of so many more!"

Whitman
CLASSICS

Five Little Peppers Midway

Freckles

Wild Animals I Have Known

Rebecca of Sunnybrook
Farm

Alice in Wonderland

Mrs. Wiggs of the
Cabbage Patch

Fifty Famous Fairy Tales

Rose in Bloom

Eight Cousins

Little Women

Little Men

Five Little Peppers and
How They Grew

Robinson Crusoe

Treasure Island

Heidi

The Call of the Wild

Tom Sawyer

Beautiful Joe

Adventures of Sherlock Holmes

Here are some of the best-loved stories of all time.
Delightful ... intriguing ... never-to-be-forgotten
tales that you will read again and again. Start
your own home library of WHITMAN CLASSICS
so that you'll always have exciting books at your
finger tips.

Whitman

REG. U.S. PAT. OFF.

Whitman ADVENTURE and MYSTERY Books

Adventure Stories for GIRLS and BOYS...

TIMBER TRAIL RIDERS

The Long Trail North
The Texas Tenderfoot
The Luck of Black Diamond

THE BOBBSEY TWINS

In the Country
Merry Days Indoors and Out
At the Seashore

DONNA PARKER

In Hollywood
At Cherrydale
Special Agent
On Her Own
A Spring to Remember
Mystery at Arawak

TROY NESBIT SERIES

The Forest Fire Mystery
The Jinx of Payrock Canyon
Sand Dune Pony

New Stories About Your Television Favorites...

Dr. Kildare
Assigned to Trouble

Janet Lennon
And the Angels
Adventure at Two Rivers
Camp Calamity

Walt Disney's Annette
The Mystery at Smugglers' Cove
The Desert Inn Mystery
Sierra Summer
The Mystery at Moonstone Bay

The Lennon Sisters
Secret of Holiday Island

Leave It to Beaver

Ripcord

The Beverly Hillbillies

Lassie
The Mystery at Blackberry Bog

Lucy
The Madcap Mystery

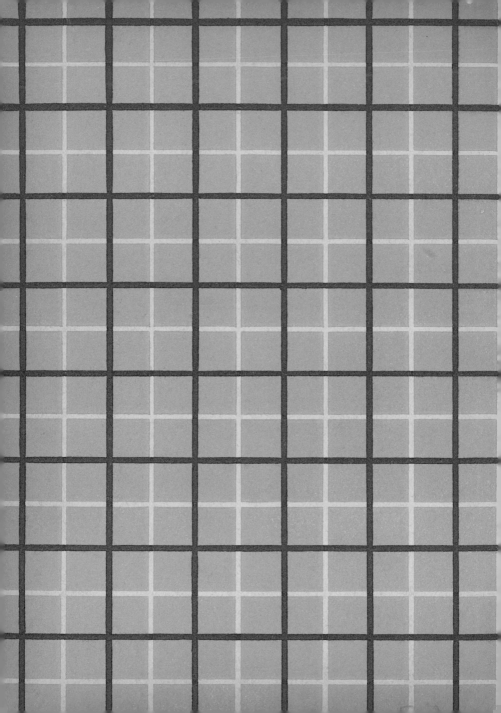